Householders

Householders

stories

KATE CAYLEY

Biblioasis
Windsor, Ontario

FIRST EDITION

10 9 8 7 6 5 4 3 2 1

Library and Archives Canada Cataloguing in Publication
Title: Householders / Kate Cayley.
Names: Cayley, Kate, author.
Description: Short stories.
Identifiers: Canadiana (print) 2021017126X | Canadiana (ebook) 20210171294 | ISBN 9781771964296 (softcover) | ISBN 9781771964302 (ebook)
Classification: LCC PS8605.A945 H68 2021 | DDC C813/.6—dc23

Edited by Daniel Wells
Copyedited by John Sweet
Text and cover designed by Michel Vrana
"Antelope with Honeycomb" collage by Allan Kausch

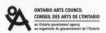

Published with the generous assistance of the Canada Council for the Arts, which last year invested $153 million to bring the arts to Canadians throughout the country, and the financial support of the Government of Canada. Biblioasis also acknowledges the support of the Ontario Arts Council (OAC), an agency of the Government of Ontario, which last year funded 1,709 individual artists and 1,078 organizations in 204 communities across Ontario, for a total of $52.1 million, and the contribution of the Government of Ontario through the Ontario Book Publishing Tax Credit and Ontario Creates.

PRINTED AND BOUND IN CANADA

Maybe it is a good thing for us to keep a few dreams of a house that we shall live in later, always later, so much later, in fact, that we shall not have time to achieve it.
—Gaston Bachelard

I instinctively sympathize with the guilty. That's my guilty secret.
—Zadie Smith

For Lea

Contents

The Crooked Man

MARTHA REGARDED HERSELF SKEPTICALLY AND assumed skepticism from the other mothers at the table. She had too many children (four), and not for a discernible reason (religion, twins), she was too young (twenty-eight), she was disordered and apologetic. She made stuffed baby toys out of felt and organic wool, her breasts leaked through old tank tops. She was blond but not seductively so: freckled and angular, snub-nosed. A child, pinkish, pedalling a bike home from a violin lesson, earnest and a little sad.

Her breasts were leaking. Denton was probably carrying their crying youngest through the house, cursing lavishly.

"I know this is going to be a difficult one, but we need to talk to the family," Bronwyn was saying, "and ask them if they can route the car somewhere else or just have her walk to the car."

Bronwyn paused, one hand tugging at a handful of her long hair, thinking. They waited.

"That might be even better, if the car was on a different street. We've got the chalk drawing on their street. And the lemonade and the bake sale. And one of the bands. *And* Martha's craft table. They'll have to understand this is a community event. It's for the whole community. I'm sure they'll understand."

"But it's her *wedding*," Martha said, louder than she meant to. "It's a shame, isn't it? It's her wedding."

Bronwyn, Marley and Alison looked at her, and she looked back at them over the table in Bronwyn's kitchen, and then down at her hands laid in front of her amidst the mugs of tea, the lists and phones and plate of cookies. Outside, she could hear Noah and Max playing.

Martha smiled often, as a cover for sleeplessness. Even though she felt the same watchful aggrieved boredom as the other mothers, she was praised for her cheerfulness. The women surrounding her, on or beside park benches, in yards and community centres, at school pickups, on her street, calling greetings from the open windows of their cars or their open screen doors, appeared to her competent and discerning. Sure of their authority, not bewildered as Martha was by having to find enough mittens to go around, by remembering to bring sunscreen to the park. They complained freely, and their complaints seemed more justified than her own. She had not endangered a career or an artistic practice in order to raise children. Her memory before Noah's birth went as far as the first half of a degree in history. After: diapers, splatters of yogurt, little jars of fruit mush, tears, mysterious stains. The other women seemed to have had more time to consider the question of what they wanted, and they had refined and elaborated on that question, as if it was a problem that could be solved.

Her own problem was Noah. Loner, lonely, prone to abrupt rage. At first, they said he was like his father, but Denton had a friendliness and self-assurance that made her shrug off the swearing, the jumpiness. Denton could not shut a door quietly. He was big, jovial, already balding, his whole back and his arms blue-black with ink. (Bronwyn had a few tasteful tattoos along her back and shoulders, delicate as leaf veins, which Martha envied; she wasn't certain enough to get something as declarative as a tattoo.) Denton drank a few beers with dinner, but it made him fond and sentimental. He roared at the children, and they laughed. He was liked. She liked him. He liked himself.

Noah was different. Thin and taut, his blue eyes frantic, his hair sticking up in light-brown tufts. At six months old he screamed if she tried to put him down, and yet being touched seemed to hurt him too. She'd dreaded changing him so much that once she'd put it off until there were red weals on his bum and the creases of his thighs. She was twenty years old.

Noah was sly now. He said mean things, cried if another child stared too hard in the playground, hit children running past. There were meetings with the teacher, the principal. Conversations in the yard that changed when Martha approached. She did not want to seem defensive; she could not defend. She lay in bed picturing his red-rimmed, too-wide eyes. He was not invited to the houses of classmates after school. He was not summoned to birthday parties. Bronwyn's son Max, a year older, was his one friend. Max enjoyed being needed, and Martha caught a whiff of patronizing kindness (Max was very like his mother), thought that Noah came home from Max's house looking furtively sad, which Martha, from experience, pretended not to see.

She trembled for Noah, she loved him, but sometimes she imagined him older, kicking someone in the face, throwing a match into the rainbow slick of a gasoline spill, in front of a stranger's quiet, sleeping house.

Outside, the boys played.

"But it's her wedding," Martha said again, more loosely.

Before she could say anything else, Max ran in with his nose bleeding, Noah eager and fearful behind him. Max had fallen off his skateboard, he'd been nowhere near Noah, and in her relief Martha forgot to bring the wedding up again.

"I'll talk to the family," Bronwyn said to Martha in the hall as they got ready to leave. "I'm sure they'll understand when I explain." She waved as they walked down the stairs.

"I feel like we live in a village," Bronwyn called to Martha, "don't you?"

Martha had never lived in a village, but she nodded, wishing for Bronwyn's confidence in her own intentions. The sun was setting.

On the way home Noah let her hold his hand and this was enough of a victory that even Denton calling out "Where the *fuck* have you been? All she wants is boob!" when she walked in the door only made her laugh and kiss him hard. He grinned at her. Ella stopped crying, smothered into her breast. And Noah was already climbing the stairs, she heard the water running as he brushed his teeth. It will be all right. She kissed Denton again. Maybe it will be all right.

It is all well-meant, Martha thinks. None of it is intended as hostility to the people who have lived in this part of Toronto since the seventies, who seem older than they are, who attend church, who wish to launch their granddaughter from the house in which she grew up, who have rented the white limousine to which she will descend, swaddled in synthetic lace on the morning of her wedding, the groom little more than a willing accessory to her temporary magnificence. The street festival has been carefully planned, and every effort has been made to include everyone, and these efforts have been made in good faith by the families who have organized it, families who have begun to buy the houses that the older people have sold, or that their children have sold after their deaths. They have moved into these small houses and they have made them beautiful according to their ideas of beauty. They have painted the walls in deep Van Gogh colours, they have exposed the red brick that was hidden under brown or yellow vinyl siding. They have laid hardwood floors and built back decks. They feel the right to stake a claim, and the street festival, the chalk drawings and sidewalk sale and music and cookies and bubble machine, are part of that claim. Few of these new people are rich, though they have the pliancy afforded by some money, they may safely accumulate modest debt. Even though Martha and Denton bought their house through an estate sale, a leaking and rotting shell of a place, even though Denton worked over every inch of it himself while they lived with his mother and Martha nursed Sam, the second of her babies, and felt sidelined and useless, the down payment was a gift from her grandmother and she knows that, however uneasy it makes her, she still falls firmly on the side of the radiant houses and the energetic educated people, who don't clip coupons even though they are daunted by the price of groceries. She knows that the world of those burnished floors and new kitchens and the world of old women bleaching their sidewalks and polishing tiles adorned with pictures of the Holy Family will not be entirely reconciled.

She looked out of the skylight that Denton had installed in their attic bedroom and listened to Denton's heavy breathing and Ella's soft whoosh, and thought of the wedding, and, on the floor below her, her three other children, Noah sleeping lightly or also awake, looking out the window. She imagined his heart beating, staccato as the ticking of a wind-up watch.

"Mama! I want you!"

Sally stood on her chair and Martha scooped her up with one arm, her other hand already stretched out for Sam's teetering glass of milk.

"Mama! I spilled!"

The glass spun on the floor. At least it hadn't shattered.

Denton had left the house early, trying to finish a job installing cabinets, working for a friend who paid him in cash, before going to his other job putting in windows and doors on the four tiny new houses down the street, squeezed onto one wide lot.

She counted to ten in her head, the way Bronwyn recommended. When that wasn't enough, she turned her back on the puddle, just in time to see Noah lift Ella down from the change table, swinging her around, her naked legs hunched against him.

"Noah! Stop!"

"She's a superhero!"

She resolved to be kind. Putting Sally down, she approached Noah.

"Give her to me, sweetie."

"She loves it!"

"She's not a toy."

"She's flying!"

"She'll pee on you!" Sam yelled from the kitchen doorway.

Noah dropped Ella, who kept her legs folded into her body, bumped her head against the floor, and lay staring at Noah in surprise.

There was a hushed moment, as if they might agree to let whatever had happened pass unmarked, though no one would, or ever did. Then Ella wailed, Martha screamed at Noah, Noah flung himself away from her and out of the room.

She sat on the couch, nursing Ella, half noticing that Sally and Sam had carefully spread three clean dishtowels over the spilled milk and left them there.

Martha collected the late slips from the school office, called *I love you* after Noah, who flinched, halfway up the stairs to his classroom, and waved one raw pink hand but did not turn back. Then she walked along Dundas Street, Ella in the sling, humming in her sleep, her forehead against Martha's chest.

Worming through the grocery list, the necessity of an evening meal, the towels she had left on the kitchen floor, was the sense she should say something to Bronwyn. She rehearsed a speech about the street party and the car that would take the bride to church. In her imaginary speech she withdrew her offer of the craft table, she provoked a disagreement that scuttled Max and Noah's friendship, she took a principled position and became subtly worthier and was left with no one to talk to, like her eldest child scanning the yard. All this happened in her head before she crossed the second light to the supermarket.

She'd stepped into the road just as she saw the young man on the bike. The bike was too small, his addict-thin body crooked over it. He wore a red bandana, track pants, a black windbreaker buttoned up to his scrawny throat. His eyes were red-veined blue, the knuckles on both hands heavily bruised. He darted in and out of traffic, his head low over the handlebars, his face rigid. She sprinted to the other side just in time, shaken. He hurtled out into the intersection, cars honking and swerving as he made it to the other side and disappeared down a side street, shouting in angry triumph at a victory she did not understand.

Denton managed to come home early. She took Noah to the pool in the community centre, leaving Denton on the edge of the playground with Ella sleeping in the stroller, Sally and Sam digging in the warm sand. She wished Denton wouldn't smoke, another thing he did that made her anxious that their family would seem unwholesome, though Denton, blowing expert rings over the back of the bench, told her that he was within his legal rights and she shouldn't care about the assholes. She couldn't help caring, felt his provocation reflected on her, not him. He appeared rakish, forgivable, his cigarette in one hand and a horror novel in the other, enjoying the spring heat wave, the sun on his face. She would be judged.

She tried to swim beside Noah, who wanted to dive and splash, affronting a stately old man who ploughed, puffing, through the deep end, so she lapped away, leaving Noah to his territory. She loved the strange order of the swimmers, the way each person found a path, rarely colliding.

She floated on her back, thinking of the man on the bike, speeding towards her as if she was not there. She watched Noah dive and hover at the bottom of the pool, fighting the buoyancy of his body, his fists clenched.

She should have sent a text first, but she couldn't decide exactly what she wanted to say (the speech in her head was out of the question), so she walked over to Bronwyn's house in the dusk, pretending to herself that she was putting Ella to sleep, gripping the stroller as she eased it onto the curb, hoping she would find Bronwyn on her porch. The porch was empty. She lifted Ella out and reached for the bell. Before she touched it, her phone rang.

"Come home right now."

They'd fought, they always fought, she thought, putting ice on the bulge on Noah's forehead. Denton was solid, Noah liquid. She should never leave them alone.

"I'm sorry."

"I know."

"I didn't think he'd—"

"I know."

As far as she could tell from competing and overlapping explanations, they'd fought about Noah's homework. Denton had yelled, Noah wept, Denton yelled louder (and he was baffled by his own anger as much as by his son, as soon as the anger left him spent and contrite). Noah ran up the stairs, Denton followed, still shouting, Noah turned back to make sure his father was watching, and then, bracing himself, he drove his forehead against the brick of the exposed chimney.

"And then he *looked* at me—"

"You weren't listening!" Noah shrieked. "You never listen!"

"—and I know I shouldn't yell—"

"Mama, it hurts—"

"I don't know what to do anymore—"

"We don't need to talk about this now," said Martha, in the voice she hated. A loving, brittle calm, the chime of maternal reassurance. She kissed Noah to the left of his bump. He passively received her kiss. The bump would be deep purple by morning.

It was eleven thirty. She wanted to go to sleep. She listened to Denton, slumped beside her, drawn into himself, talking without looking at her. He was failing, he knew he was failing, a failure, he said, of love or patience. What if he was not the right father for this barbed child, what if he could not help Noah, what if neither of them could? She listened, thinking of how jolly Denton seemed, how easy with himself, how surprised her neighbours would be if she described him now. The way he stared at the cluttered shelf on the opposite wall, at their clothes overflowing the laundry basket, the way he seemed on the point of tears. She listened until he stopped talking. He fell asleep before she did, unburdened if not absolved, perhaps grateful for her permission to show himself at a loss. His arm, slung casually across her waist, grew heavier. Her eyes were dry as sand. She turned away from him to Ella, who clawed at the sheet, looking for milk.

"You came to my house?" Bronwyn asked the next day as they walked together from the school doors.

"You saw me?"

"Max said he saw you come up the steps."

Bronwyn stopped walking, absently jingling her house keys in one hand. Martha fought an urge to go out the gate, to refuse explanations.

"I got a call. Noah—you know."

Bronwyn touched her shoulder, nodding.

"Can we sit?" Martha asked.

They sat on a bench.

"Are you okay?" Bronwyn asked, her brow creased. "I mean, you seem—are you really okay?"

"I'm fine."

"Noah?"

"Noah's fine." She sounded angry without meaning to. Then she felt angry. "I think we need to move all the stuff off that street."

"What street?"

"The street where Zalia's wedding is."

"Zalia?"

"The bride."

A short pause.

"Oh—you mean—oh. No, Zalia's the grandmother. The bride is Ashley."

Another pause. If I was Bronwyn, Martha thought, I would make a joke, I would turn this into a joke and make us both laugh.

"I'm sorry. I've thought about this a lot. I think it isn't fair to make her walk to the car."

"Fair?"

"I know it's supposed to be for everyone, and it is, I know it is, I can see that, I agree with you, but it isn't really, I don't think it is, I think we need to move everything over, or I'm not going to do it, the craft table I mean, I can't, I can't."

"I'm sorry you feel that way."

"I do. I do."

"It would be a loss."

Martha wasn't going to cry, she wished she could, even if crying was the way women threw punches.

"But I talked to them," Bronwyn was saying, "I've already talked to them."

"When?"

"Yesterday. To Zalia."

"She doesn't speak English, I thought."

"I speak Portuguese. My mother was from Lisbon. Did I never say?"

Martha shook her head. She was too humiliated to speak.

"I thought I told you that. Of course, the dialect is slightly different. They don't mind. Really they don't. Anyway, no one's making her walk to the car. How did you get that idea? She'll just be picked up a little earlier, that's all. A scenic route to church."

Ella mercifully woke up, was lifted out, cooed over.

"I miss that age. You're lucky. All those babies."

"Yes."

"You shouldn't worry so much. You have so much to worry about. If you'd rather not run the craft table—"

"No, no—"

"Maybe that would be better anyway. You have so much on your plate."

"It's fine."

Martha sounded angry again. She didn't know how to stop.

"I do wonder if it would be better. For the whole thing. If we didn't have it. I've been thinking. Maybe better to skip it? It's such a generous offer, but those things can be so messy."

"I don't mind."

"I think it might be a better choice not to have a craft table. Maybe next year. When you're less overstretched."

This was final, Martha could see. Bronwyn got up, frowned at her keys. Martha remained on the bench.

"We should really get the boys together. Maybe next weekend?"

"That would be great."

"Saturday? No, wait, Max has a birthday party. Sunday morning?"

She made herself walk home along a different route, past the controversial house. She thought of the bride, whose name was not Zalia. She could barely picture her. Whereas Bronwyn knew her grandmother, probably knew some of the details of her life. Am I like Noah, Martha thought, miscalculating the world? Seeing malevolence where there is none?

The stroller caught in a crack in the sidewalk, she stumbled and cursed as loudly as Denton, and as she recovered, she thought she saw, behind the yellow curtains of the tired bungalow, a flicker of interest, a pair of peering eyes.

She put the ready squares of cotton away, stuffed the finished animals into a bag in the backroom, which was full of boxes and empty bottles and jars, mismatched things, postponed things. Her for-later room, when there was time. And she'd still be young, when she found time to finish all her projects, to sort and divest. Bronwyn had been forty when Max was born, but she could get Ella launched on the school system and still be young. She gave an oddly proportioned rabbit a punch, knotted the bag.

She'd embroidered the animals with red and blue thread, and they had black beads for eyes. She'd kept them simple: these were models, to show the children how to do it. Another time. And she could always give them as Christmas presents, or new-baby presents. They were sturdy and artless. But the beads were too shiny. It made the animals look cunning. She would snip the beads off and embroider complicated and beautiful eyes, friendly brown eyes, with fine lines of thread for lashes.

Bronwyn was right anyway, Martha thought, on the day of the festival. She could never have managed it. Sally had the flu and was home with Denton, watching a movie. It was too hot to fiddle with stuffing, guide small sweaty fingers. She had very little sympathy to spare when it was this hot. She would have spoken sharply to other people's children, been impatient at their disappointment when the thing they'd imagined and the thing they had made didn't match.

The streets were crowded. It was hard to push the stroller without seeming rude. She kept losing sight of Noah and Sam, briefly panicking before spotting a flash of familiar T-shirt, the back of a head. Swaths of the neighbourhood were cordoned off; she saw Emily, Alison's youngest daughter, leaping from the curb to the road and back. Martha was afraid of cars, and had made her children afraid (she was also afraid of strangers, highways, crosswalks, airplanes, and other, less tangible things), but Emily's glee was sad. As if Martha, Alison, all of them, were raising children so obedient that a sanctioned deviation, as small as skipping from the curb to the street, was the closest they could come to rebellion. There was a mythical kingdom, somewhere in her head, in which her children and the children she saw every day ran loose in open fields, built structures out of discarded wood and rusted nails, like the clips she sometimes watched on YouTube of rural communes in the seventies, in which grubby, jubilant children toiled beside their hoeing parents or helped out in a makeshift dairy. She knew that those places had been full of infighting, that the food had run low, that many of those children had grown up eager to move to cities and assert their private and precious identity, insulating themselves with their houses and possessions. Denton's brother's tight-lipped ex-wife had grown up in a commune in Maine, and her stories did not make Martha envious. But there was something about that time that made her feel that she had cocooned and shortchanged her own children through a failure of nerve. Maybe that would have saved Noah, she thought, catching sight of him standing alone, and then wondered why she thought he was already lost.

They ate fish and chips on the sidewalk before pushing their way on into the park. Bronwyn had made a dance for the end of the evening, working with volunteers, some professional dancers like herself, some not, and a choir made up of neighbourhood people. It was growing dark when the audience gathered, sitting on the steep side of the hill looking down into the soccer field.

The soccer field was edged with huge white paper lanterns. It was a still evening; they did not move in the wind. Noah sat on one side of Martha, Sam on the other, Ella slept. The waiting people quieted, the park darkened. As the daylight emptied out, the lanterns grew bigger, solemn. Music began: something instrumental, familiar, a blurred soft-industrial pulse looped, and a row of white lights came on at the far side of the field, Christmas lights probably, or smaller versions of the paper lanterns.

When the lights came on, Martha saw a row of people sitting on the pavement where the parking lot met the grass. It looked like forty or fifty people. Companionably close to each other but not touching, men and women and children, all wearing pale shirts and grey pants or skirts, and brown ties. They looked across the soccer field at the audience and smiled. Then they stood and began walking slowly over the half-lit grass. The formation broke—some people came forward, some held back, some walked to one side while others continued straight ahead, and a few people sat abruptly down on the ground.

As she watched, the sheer size of the group, their deliberate movements, their hesitations and digressions, began to be beautiful. Closer, the people lost the look of clones. Max was there, solid and formal, moving slightly out of step. Marley, holding her daughter's hand, a glint of grey in her hair. Martha recognized more people, surprising people: the man who owned the convenience store, an older woman who lived alone on Martha's street and who was so hostile to the children that they called her a witch, but here she looked frail and heartfelt, walking in time to the music, looking out over the heads of the watchers.

The music stopped. The dancers kept moving, spread farther over the grass. Then Martha saw the choir, standing to one side by a big tree. They were dressed in the same uniform, but they were all old, a little stooped, deep lines creasing their faces. And they began to sing.

Do you realize that you have the most beautiful face?

Martha cried. Not much, no falling tears, just a few small pricks around her eyelids.

She didn't turn her head to see if she was the only person who cried, but for the moment Noah was not lost, he was beside her, they were together with all these people, that was why Bronwyn had made this dance, so that Martha and everyone else would believe, if only for the duration of it, that they were not alone, that was the point of the dance. Wasn't it?

Do you realize that everyone you know someday will die?

She saw Bronwyn afterwards, standing in a little knot of people. Her broad face, her dark hair foaming over her bony shoulders. She was hugging one of the dancers, closing her eyes as she held the woman, and Martha saw she was crying benevolently, like it was nothing. She wanted to thank Bronwyn for the dance, but whatever Martha had seen now seemed to have nothing to do with Bronwyn, surrounded by her admirers, sure of herself. Martha didn't want to tell her anything.

She got up from the grass, she took her children home.

When she saw Bronwyn next, it was Monday, and both were worn down by the weekend, the long stretch of Sunday after the party. A spattering of confetti still clung to the church steps, but Martha had seen the grandmother going into her house with her groceries. She wondered if Ashley had left for her honeymoon, and tried to picture her, but could only imagine scratchy white lace, the swooping train of a cheap wedding dress.

Bronwyn hugged her. "Come have a coffee."

Martha hesitated, then agreed.

They walked towards the café Bronwyn liked, and Bronwyn did not mention the wedding or the craft table or the dance, and Martha was grateful. Noah had had one of his dreams again, in which something was chasing him. When he had this dream, he screamed in his sleep and for a long time afterwards, held between them, his body knotted and wary. She wondered if it dated from the nursery rhyme, read to him years earlier, before she realized how careful she had to be.

There was a crooked man

And he walked a crooked mile
He found a crooked sixpence
Upon a crooked stile
He bought a crooked cat
Which caught a crooked mouse …

This man staggered through Noah's mind and sometimes broke to the surface, grinning, reaching out thin arms.

"I really loved the dance."

"Thanks, thanks so much, that means a lot to me."

She is going to say something, Martha thought. When they reached the café, and sat curling their hands around the mugs. Bronwyn would cut her out. Cut Noah out.

Crossing the street, they both saw him. The young man on the bike, angular, already broken, threading his way through the cars, in pursuit of something she couldn't see, or pursued. Or both at once, a nightmare, caught in a nightmare. She grabbed Bronwyn's arm to pull her back onto the pavement but before he reached them he swerved into the oncoming lane and was hit by a white van.

As he flew into the air, Martha sensed the same hush she felt before she screamed at one of her children, a lull in which it might still be possible for his unhappy body not to meet the road.

Bronwyn ran forward and held his head as another driver got out and dialed 911, and the man in the van stumbled onto the pavement.

"He came at me. He just came at me."

Martha found herself taking the man's arm, supporting him.

"Is he—is he dead?"

"No."

"He's dead." His voice shook.

"No. No, he's not."

"I killed him."

"No."

Blood ran over Bronwyn's lap.

"I fucking killed him."

"No. No."

Sirens, getting nearer, ambulance, fire, police, then two paramedics and three firefighters surrounded the form lying in the road. Martha couldn't see Bronwyn through the huddle, and then Bronwyn was led away. Another paramedic covered her shoulders with a blanket.

Martha stayed with the driver. He was grey under his stubble, his hands working together, his whole body trembling. It wasn't his fault, but he would think it was, if he was a decent man. Even if it wasn't true. The crooked man was lifted onto a stretcher and into one of the ambulances, which sped away. Maybe they would be able to save him, Martha thought. I can't. I can't.

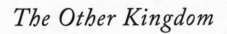

The Other Kingdom

NAOMI AND HER FRIEND CAROL STOOD BESIDE A MEMO-
rial in the square of a town in Maine. They were seeing America,
and so had no single destination and no end point. Carol was
hoping to write an essay about protest movements and the
Vietnam War. Naomi was hoping to find a new life. The different scope of their expectations had begun to grate. For weeks
they had slept in Carol's car and eaten mostly fruit and crackers.
They filled white plastic canisters with water at gas stations. The
water sloshed onto their feet. The crackers were small and dry
and Carol said they reminded her of the host. Naomi chewed
and didn't answer. She was still called Nancy then.

She'd made them drive to San Francisco to hear Jim Jones
preach love and revolution. But he and his followers frightened
her—his purple satin robes, his promises to raise the dead. The
crowd sat on folding chairs in an auditorium with armed men
posted on either side of the door. The people sitting around
Naomi and Carol cried and were saved. Naomi felt only embar-
rassment at the young women gazing up at the stage, stretching
their hands out, hoping he would look at them. Naomi was

easily embarrassed by anything that felt like sexual hysteria and intelligent enough to know that salvation would not be easy, even though she wanted it to be. It helped to have Carol beside her in a state of furious refusal, her arms wrapped around herself at the sight of the guns. They did not stay for the meal. Before they left San Francisco, they visited an upstart ashram in Golden Gate Park. Carol sat primly on a bench, ignored greetings from stoned young men. Nancy ducked into a hut and was sloppily blessed by a dirty white man dressed in rags, then hectored on the inner light by a heavy-set older white woman who referred to herself as Mother. Nancy waited to feel something. She didn't. She walked back out into the sunlight and called Carol uptight for not going in, though she hadn't expected her to. She followed Carol to protests, and watched Carol write notes into a series of spiral pads, but, unlike Carol, she did not want to set off a bomb in a government office or lie down under advancing rows of boots. Carol didn't really want that either, but she pretended to. She wanted to write essays.

Wherever they went, Nancy sought out anything that promised drastic and essential wisdom. Fortune tellers, meetings on liberation theology, churches set up in abandoned storefronts. Everything was treated as a possible site of revelation, from revolutionary manifestos pressed into her hands at protests to messages chalked on walls in alleyways. But now they'd found their way back nearer the border, and every quest had come up empty. She didn't want to go home yet. She'd determined she didn't have a home.

Carol was worried about money. Naomi didn't think much about what would happen when they ran out, but there was very little left, even with living off crackers and the apples they stole from orchards at night. Once, Carol bit into a soft wriggling worm, spat out the car window, gagging. Naomi laughed at her and she laughed too, both of them overwhelmed by the empty road and the stars. This surprised Carol by turning out to be one of her happiest memories of that time, perhaps of her life, up there with the day they jumped into a public fountain after watching a group of young men burn draft cards. They sat together on the lip of the fountain as the crowd, now the spectacle was over, broke into smaller clusters or drifted away. The angel at the centre of the fountain presided. Naomi cupped her hands in the shallow water, drank.

"You'll get sick."

"I'm thirsty. Try it."

The bottom of the fountain was slick with algae.

"No thanks."

Naomi stood up, balancing on the stone edge. "Come in with me?"

"You're crazy."

Carol wished immediately she hadn't spoken; it sounded like a dare.

Naomi jumped, slipped, righted herself. The water only came to her knees.

"Come in. Come in."

Carol crossed her arms. "No."

"You're scared."

"I'm *not*," Carol said, dismayed by the childish pitch of her own voice.

"Then come in."

Carol stood and stepped into the water, gasping with the cold. "There. Happy?"

But Naomi wasn't looking at her anymore, she was moving towards the angel in the centre of the fountain, ripples in her wake.

"Where are you going?"

"In," she said. Knelt. Lay back. The water closed over her head.

Carol waited, shivering.

Naomi came up, lifting her arms. "Do I look like the angel?"

The water streamed down like wings, it was true, but Carol was too cold and exasperated to admit it.

"No. You look freezing."

"I am."

"What am I supposed to do if you get sick?"

"Watch me!" She lay back again, grabbing Carol's ankle with one hand, and Carol kicked her away.

For the rest of her life, Carol remembered Nancy lying back the second time. Her eyes open under the water, bubbles gathering around her mouth and nose. Her dark hair turned green and weedy.

The memory of Nancy in the fountain was clearer than Carol's memory of the young man who was listening from the other side of the monument in the small Maine town while they argued about where to go next. Carol thought they should hire themselves out to farmers (neither of them knew anything about farming, but the idea seemed noble and practical), earn some more cash (she wasn't sure if they had enough left for gas), then drive back to Toronto.

"I think we should stay longer."

Naomi didn't think it, she had decided it, Carol could see. "Why?"

"I have a hunch."

"I want to get home."

Carol frowned. Nancy smiled. She had not told Carol that she had no home; Carol would not have understood and was always demanding explanations. Carol did not want to baptize herself in a fountain. She did not believe in a new life. Naomi remembered their friendship was circumstantial and improbable. She smiled maddeningly.

Mattie chose that moment to appear from behind the monument. He stopped in front of them, looking sure of his welcome. Jeans and a stained white T-shirt, brown eyes latticed with gold, crooked teeth in shades of ivory yellow. Later, renamed Naomi, she poeticized that Mattie's teeth stood in for the difference between them: the affluent kindness of her parents, his mean childhood. Her white, even teeth.

Mattie offered a smudgy flyer to the girl who smiled. Nancy noticed that the tip of his little finger was missing.

"Aren't you going to read it?" he asked.

She looked at the flyer. A rough woodcut of a sun and stars above a boat full of animals (her childhood home so secular that she did not immediately recognize the ark) and, in block letters, JOHN WILL GIVE A SERMON, then an address in the town and that night's date. Looking up, there was the face of the boy (he was two years younger than she was, and would look like a boy at forty, though she no longer knew him then).

"Will you come?"

"Probably not," she said, in a voice that he did not realize was teasing.

"But you have to come!" he said, distressed.

Carol looked away.

"Why?" Nancy asked.

"Because you need to hear him. I can see it. I can see it in your face."

This was something he said often, and believed, but Nancy didn't know that.

Very softly, he put one hand on her wrist. He held it there, as though feeling for her pulse.

"Please come."

She blushed easily.

"I'll see you there!" he called, and, grinning at the fact of the sun and the warm morning and himself, he left her with the flyer in her hand.

Two years earlier, Nancy moved her bag off the seat beside her to make room for Carol when she ran in late to her first history lecture at the University of Toronto. Seventeen, they were a year younger than most of their classmates, marked in their own minds as especially brilliant, though Carol's brilliance was harder-won. Her parents owned a small grocery store and held her in perplexed awe. Nancy had the listless ease of someone entering into an inheritance. Her parents both taught English literature (her mother's area was poetry, her father's, novels, both happily entrenched in the nineteenth and early twentieth centuries), and she had decided on history in order to avoid their orbit. She could dismiss the green lawns and the trees in the philosopher's walk, which Carol quickly learned to do as well while secretly loving the feel of the grey stone under her hand, the sense of her own arrival. She would steal the keys to the kingdom that Nancy had been born holding. Raised in a squeaky bungalow and embarrassed by her mother's pride in the new linoleum, Carol, invited to Nancy's house, was amazed by what Nancy took for granted: books over-spilling from floor-to-ceiling shelves, conversations at meals.

Carol's childhood, it seemed to her now that she was leaving it, had been spent staring dutifully at her own pewter pencil marks on a series of cheap notebooks, her legs twisted around the crosspieces of a shiny kitchen chair. Around her, her mother's heavy cotton lace doilies in pinks, yellows, blues. A shrine to the Virgin, who simpered above the sink. Carol's mother lit candles at Mary's feet, offered prayers for the other children that ought to have followed Carol, if only to relieve her parents of the burden of her stubborn cleverness. But after Carol, there was nothing.

The messy confidence of Nancy's house disoriented her. Crooked carpets on bare floors, dust drifting in corners, tea leaves slopped into the drain, as though that was how people ought to live, right down to the perilously overgrown backyard, with its leaning trees and bare patches of earth. Nancy's parents both drank, but not as Carol's father did, defiantly, watched by his wife with conventional disapproval. Harold and Ellen, as Carol was immediately invited to call them, poured each other drinks and Harold set his sweating tumbler down on the coffee table, where it left a ring that he wiped with his undone cuff, still talking. Ellen raised her eyebrows at Carol, as though he were a joke between them, as though Carol were an adult in an adult world of books and jokes and marks left by whiskey glasses.

Carol, wanting to please Nancy, soon learned to feel impatience with Nancy's parents, with their welcome and their snobberies and their enthusiasm for everything that did not interest her own parents. She wanted neither world. She was learning scorn, learning to refer to herself as working-class as a way to win an argument, more covertly learning that she was in love with Nancy, which was delicious and terrifying, something she could barely allow herself to think and would never be able to say.

Nancy was an only child by design. She had been told so often, particularly when she was difficult. More children would have disturbed her parents' guarded and circumscribed trajectories. The house was, for a child, very lonely. Her parents worked in their studies at opposites ends of the upstairs hall, mildly shut their doors against her. She walked to school alone in her un-ironed uniform, quotations running through her head. *My mother groaned, my father wept/Into the dangerous world I leapt.* Her parents were amused by her seriousness, exasperated by her intensity. But Nancy would learn to be satisfied. She would grow up.

When Nancy was nine, her father took her to see *On the Beach,* and then to a diner he loved, where he sliced his eggs into little squares and told her about nuclear annihilation.

"But will it happen?" she asked.

He looked at his fork, swallowed his mouthful. "I don't know. I hope not."

"But what if it does?"

"*Enjoy yourself, enjoy yourself, it's later than you think,*" he sang into her shocked face. He did not mean to be cruel. He'd been alive long enough to decide that personal happiness was as high as he could reach, and that everything else was hubris and despair. He thought that was the only answer he could give a frightened child. It was the only honest answer he had.

She drank her milkshake. She thought about the survivors in the film, restrained in their grief, waiting on the Australian beaches for the cloud to reach them. Going to parties, falling in love, enjoying the speed of fast cars or the soft depths of couches, but really just waiting for the poison that would come on the air as soon as the winds shifted, poison that had already wiped out all other life on earth. She tried to recall the speech of the young mother who, finally conceding that there is no escape and she can at least choose the hour of her death, allows her husband to give them both a white powder to drink before they lie down side by side in bed, chaste as brother and sister, the baby in the crib sucking on a lethal bottle.

"I'd like that cup of tea now," she whispered, putting down the milkshake. Her father touched her hand across the table. He suspected he should have chosen a different film, but he liked Fred Astaire and Gregory Peck, he wanted her to share what he liked.

That night, they woke to screams. He ran down the hall with Ellen behind him. Nancy was sitting up in bed. Her eyes were wide open but they couldn't tell if she was really awake. The sound was shattering. They held her, they shook her, she finally collapsed in Harold's arms. Her parents looked at each other, helpless and wordless. They persuaded her to shut her eyes and watched till she grew quiet and slept, or pretended to sleep.

She had seen them look at each other. They were hypocrites and the world was full of hypocrites and Nancy would not allow them to convince her that hypocrisy was a form of bravery. When she thought of her childhood, she believed that was the moment she knew, without knowing, that she would leave them entirely. She would find the dangerous world. *I leapt, I leapt*, she thought, crouched under her desk during bomb drills. Waiting for a sign. A few years after that, she demanded that her parents read the Port Huron Statement. *Our work is guided by the sense that we may be the last generation in the experiment with living.*

But she went to university and met Carol and walked slowly in marches and wore a black arm band for the Viet Cong and joined committees and asked what she could do to help draft dodgers and lectured her parents and moved with Carol and other less significant people into a house with a weedy yard to the south of Bloor (not so far from where she'd grown up, but to her a momentous crossing, like the tracks or the river) and got moderately high in the living room, staring at the prism hung in the window, and washed her hair over the sink with harsh Castile soap and sat cross-legged on the floor at various meetings, and still the world continued on, frustratingly elsewhere. The people around her spoke earnestly, were intelligent and good, but she thought they would turn into some version of her parents. Sure of their place in a world they had altered, though not enough. This could not be all there was.

Perhaps she had arrived too late. Perhaps she was in the wrong country. In other places, other countries, there had been a stream of bright flashes. Explosions, immolations. A student in Prague poured gas over his head and struck a match, ran screaming with the flames flapping behind him. An old librarian in Detroit soaked herself in kerosene and sat burning on the pavement, her hands folded like the Buddhist monks she emulated. The monks themselves, upright in their implacable orange bloom. Stutter of guns at Kent State, dead students on the lawn that looked like the lawns Nancy walked beside on her way to class. Two more at Jackson State, young men tumbled on bloody earth. Nancy dreamed in flames. She wrote essays on *The Waste Land* (*Shall I at least set my lands in order?*), grew a garden in the backyard of the communal house (which was chaotic and dirty in a way that would have been too much even for her parents, who had a cleaning lady in every two weeks to restore calm), played Doc Sinclair and The Incredible String Band albums over and over, driving Carol crazy, underlined passages in novels with a stubby blue pen. None of it was enough. None of it was the life she was seeking. In her room she wept for desolation, her windows open to the night.

She handed in the essay and finished her exams and was sitting in her room when Carol knocked on her door and asked her to come with her, to drive across the border and see everything they were missing. *The Hangman's Beautiful Daughter* was playing in the background.

Lay down my dear sister
Won't you lay and take your rest?

Won't you lay your head upon your saviour's breast?
And I love you, but Jesus loves you the best
And I bid you goodnight, goodnight, goodnight

Nancy said yes. She packed a canvas bag and emptied her bank account.

"I guess this is it," Nancy said.

The rain that had threatened all afternoon hit as they shut the door behind them. The day had turned cold and they'd been aimless, quarrelsome. Just before coming to find the house, Nancy goaded Carol into spending some of their dwindling money at a diner, where they ate hamburgers and drank cups of weak coffee and talked hilariously, restored by caffeine and meat. The loudly made-up waitress slid the bill along the table. They noticed for the first time that the other tables were empty, that a boy was mopping the floor around them. They were in a small town where everyone went home at night and they laughed more as they left, leaning against each other, and pulled their jackets closed, their faces pinched against the wind.

Some chairs stood against the wall, leaflets and books piled on them. A plastic bucket plinked from a leak in the ceiling, yellowish water brimmed at the rim.

There was a fanlight above the door, and a fluorescent strip flickered on the ceiling, but the hallway had an underwater dimness to it. They went to the open door at the end of the hall. About thirty people around Nancy's age sat at the feet of an old man. Some mats and blankets were spread out on the speckled grey floor. A little heat came off the bodies, but the room itself resisted warmth. A tray of incense burned behind the man. Some of the people were wrapped in the blankets, their intent heads rising above the brown wool. Thin cloth was draped over the windows, candles clustered in corners, stuck in bottles or leaning in glasses; there was a sweet smell of melted wax, and some black singe marks on the beige paint, a large burn spread over one patch of the floor.

The man, John, sat in the only chair, a lamp set beside him on a blue plastic crate, the top of the shade covered with a white cloth. Nancy guessed that she and Carol were the only outsiders from the way people turned to look at them, then turned back. She saw Mattie, who raised his hand. He sat beside John, on a wooden stool that had once been a spool for industrial cable, cocooned in a purple shawl fringed with beads. He folded his hands in his lap. Nancy and Carol crouched down near the door. Carol had already made up her mind, Nancy could tell. She knew what to expect and would not be surprised.

What surprised Nancy, transcending the mundane smell and feel of the room, the poise of those expectant bodies, was John. He was probably in his early fifties, not really old, but his hair was white, in uncombed clumps around his face, resolving into a grey goat-beard. His skin was reddened, rough in places. She guessed he was familiar with sleeping outdoors, but it seemed beautiful to her, the layers of his skin apparent, separated into pinks, yellows, greys. He nodded at her. He had been expecting her.

She told her daughter that her life had begun in that moment, that she was truly seen for the first time. By then she'd become someone who used phrases like *truly seen* as a way to reassure herself. She'd made a habit of overemphasis, wanting everything that followed to be destiny. The daughter wanted the same thing. They regarded each other, firelight on the walls of the room where they lived, with others, in a farmhouse on the edge of the American woods.

"Are we going to just sit here?" Carol whispered, fidgeting.

John cleared his throat, spat on the floor beside him.

"Fair enough, sweetheart," he said. His voice was low and a little hoarse. "Anyway, I've only got a few things to say. We all talk too much. Even me."

Later that night, Nancy sat at the kitchen table of the house farther outside the town where John lived with his followers. Mattie heated soup over the stove. The kitchen was dark, one oil lamp in the centre of the table. He brought her a bowl and watched her eat as though he wanted nothing more than to sit across from her at midnight as she spooned vegetable broth into her mouth. Everyone else had gone to bed, which confused Nancy, who thought she was coming to some kind of party, maybe to hear another sermon, something that would prolong the night. John had kissed her forehead and said he hoped to see her in the morning. She blushed and didn't answer. Mattie told her about the first time he'd heard John speak.

That was a year earlier, sitting behind the stair railings with his best friend Charlie. The boys had bruised faces, from roughhousing with each other, both unappealingly high from whatever they could lay their hands on, which wasn't much. A mixture of weed and cough syrup, chased with whiskey.

John arrived at the house Mattie lived in with his grandparents. John was the son of their recently deceased landlord, owed a year of rent. Since the letter informing his grandparents of the death, this visit had been obsessively expected, and Mattie's grandfather imagined their eviction, sometimes in his nightly drunkenness describing how he would defend himself with a shotgun (which he did not own). Mattie's grandmother ignored him, turning to her shelves cumbered with knick-knacks, the china shepherdesses she collected from Tetley tins.

Until Mattie's grandmother let John into the house, they thought he was a hobo or a Jehovah's Witness, in his shabby, over-large suit, his white hair springing around his head. John had not seen his father in more than twenty years and did not know what to do with his inheritance. He wandered, had most recently washed up in Boston, where he railed against war, slept on a mattress on the floor of an otherwise empty room, an oddity in a house full of young radicals. The basement was full of guns, which did not interest him very much, though he conceded they might be necessary.

When the letter came informing him of his father's death (months after the fact, he was hard to find), John bought a suit, washed himself in the blistered tub, and took the train to New Haven, where he met with his father's lawyer, who reminded him of the existence of that other house, which his father had inherited and he himself had never seen, with tenants who were far behind in rent. He took an early bus to Mattie's town with the house deed in his pocket.

He had an address but no directions, and he would not ask for help from anyone he saw. He walked through the streets, eating apples from a paper bag and throwing the cores into the road. It was afternoon when he found the house.

An old woman answered the door. She was wearing a frayed housedress, her feet swollen in lilac-coloured slippers. He told her who he was.

"May I come in?"

She shifted, wanting to refuse, then stood aside, still partly in the doorway so he had to enter sideways. He followed her into the kitchen, the only room with a light on.

There was a pile of dishes in the sink. The floor was slightly sticky, the walls the light green of a hospital or school, decorated with mean-spirited Biblical quotations.

The wages of sin is death.

I am the Way, the Truth, and the Life, no man may come unto the Father but by me.

Vengeance is mine, sayeth the Lord.

An old man sat at the table with his back to them. The woman hesitated.

"Bill, this is the man that owns the house."

Bill's grin was bloated, his eyes red-rimmed, burgundy spiderwebs across his nose and cheeks. He stood up, a head shorter than John, held out his hand. John could feel ridges where two of the fingers had been broken.

"I'm sorry about your dad."

"Thank you."

The woman began to make tea. There was an arthritic deliberateness to her movements as she set out the cups, paused before she lifted the canister down.

She knocked one of the cups off the counter. It did not break. She stood looking at it. John picked up the cup and held it out to her. When she did not take it, he placed it back on the counter.

"When do you want us out?" she said.

"Out?"

"Of the *house*."

"Why—why would I want you out?"

"The *rent*."

"Shut up," Bill said.

"The rent?"

"We kept thinking maybe he forgot, we didn't think he was dead. I've got family we could go to, but it's hard, it's hard, we got our grandson, and I want to be in my house—"

"I told you to shut up," Bill said.

"You don't have to leave your house."

There was a silence. John could see two teenaged boys sitting behind the banisters.

The kettle shrilled. She snatched it off the stove, put it down again, wincing.

"God, you'd think you'd remember to use the damn oven mitt," Bill said, "it's right there."

She meekly put on the mitt, poured, set the tea in front of them. She stayed standing.

"Right there," Bill repeated, lighting a cigarette.

She looked to John like milkweed in the middle of winter, rattled. Bill hit her, John thought. But when she died, Bill would tell anyone who would listen, even strangers, that she had been more than he deserved. A saint, an angel. He had that face.

Mattie, on the stairs, waited to see who would speak next.

"So what do we do now, mister?"

"John."

"John. What do we do now?"

John drew an envelope out of his jacket pocket. "I am going to give you this house."

Bill's hand trembled around the cigarette. Mattie had never imagined his grandfather could be so disconcerted. His grandfather did not stand down. He'd seen him kick in a door. Sometimes he'd been on the other side of it. It was wonderful to see him like this.

"You must be nuts, mister," Bill said.

John opened the envelope and spread the deed out on the table. Mattie wished he would turn around again so he could see his face. But then he began to speak.

Mattie knew that John was speaking to him. Neither of his grandparents seemed able to listen, hypnotized by the deed under John's hand. John told them, without looking at them, about his first vision, when he was trapped in a burning church in Italy, long ago, centuries ago it seemed to Mattie. He shook his head to clear it.

"… And so I went to the desert, there I was in the desert, stumbling through the sand, I was saved but I was still lost, in millions of years of sand, and it was cold in the night, cold as a crater on the moon, but I had such evil in me, I was going down into the darkness in which we are made, so I could find my people, I will know them when I find them, that's why I move from place to place, seeking."

Mattie could see he frightened himself. But Mattie was not afraid.

"Well, you're nuts, mister," Bill said again.

"Yes," John said, "I know."

He stood, and signed the deed over, and went.

Mattie and Charlie got up and followed him.

All the way to the bus station, where John sat down on a bench outside. Mattie and Charlie stayed by the door. Lighting cigarettes, they flicked the ashes into the evening dark. Mattie could not think how to speak to him.

"Hello," John said.

They fumbled ineptly with their cigarettes until Mattie threw his into the street to show he'd made a decision.

"Take me with you," he said.

"So John says it was like we were Adam, *and Adam walked with God in the cool of the evening*. We were lost, sitting in that bus station, and we knew it then. It got dark and we got on the bus with him, just in the clothes we had. He was waiting a long time for us. For anyone. Who could ask to be saved."

Nancy set the spoon down beside her empty bowl. Mattie put his hand over her wrist, the same gesture as that morning.

It was easy, suddenly, to ask to be saved. As easy as she'd hoped it would be.

"You live in the belly of the beast, you good people," John said, "whether you want to or not, you sell yourselves to the progress culture and the development culture, giving you a metal body in place of the good body you were born with, making you flip switches until your hands are curved to the shape of a switch. I tell you, you crazy young people, you're all nuts for Mao, but he wants you to be a cog in the wheel that never rusts. But why be a cog in the wheel? For better wheels and better systems and better machines until we are parts in a machine that can't die? We must make small things now, we must find where we can be foolish and slow and move slowly into the light. Why should there not be prophets? Why should we be always waiting for the promised land? When God is just an ordinary guy, who walks with you already, not as some pretty boy in a stained glass window, but in the work of your hands. Don't worry, folks, I'm not getting holy-roller, I'm not going to whip out a book full of rules. Christ was all virtue, and acted from impulse, not from rules."

Marriage of Heaven and Hell, Nancy thought, her parents' house, the smell of paper and spoiled milk.

Mattie, whose name she did not yet know, rang a brass bell, and a young woman with long brown braids picked her way through the seated listeners, offering each person bread from a basket. The brass bell rang at intervals.

"Let's go," Carol whispered in her ear, "I think I got the gist."

"You go," Nancy said, "I'll find you later."

Carol hesitated, then scrambled up.

Nancy could hear the rush of rain as Carol opened the door, cut off again as it shut behind her. She did not wonder where Carol would go, in the rain, moving down the empty street back to the car, not knowing what to do next.

Nancy finished her bread. It was good. She didn't want to get the gist. The man with the missing fingertip was smiling.

"Come sit by me," John said.

Nancy didn't think of what the last two days had been for Carol, who had walked back the morning after the meeting to the house where John had given his sermon and found it unlocked and empty. Crusts of wax on the floor of the room the only sign that anything had happened there.

Carol had stood in the cold room, wishing someone would come in, someone who could tell her what to do. She didn't know anyone in the town. There was no one to ask where the man and his followers might have gone. She walked through the streets all that day and the next, her arms crossed, rubbing the rough skin of her elbow. She didn't believe in calling police. She thought about calling Nancy's parents. She had ludicrous moments of wanting to call her own mother. But then Nancy tapped on the window, where Carol was huddled with her chin on her knees, pretending to read the SCUM *Manifesto*, her eyes tracing the same sentences over and over.

"I thought you were dead."

"I'm fine. I'm really good."

"I thought you were dead. I thought you were *dead*."

Carol got out of the car. She wanted to scream or cry, but Nancy appeared radiant and not even a little ashamed. Beautiful and indifferent, holding something in her hand, which she offered to Carol.

"This is for you."

"What is it?" Carol asked stupidly, hoping for an apology, an explanation, something that would take back Nancy's certainty.

"It's for my parents. So you don't need to tell them anything. I want to make this easier for you."

"Make what easier?"

"I'm staying here."

Carol was silent. There had to be an explanation now. There wasn't.

"What do you mean? I just leave you here?"

"You can go home without me. I won't mind."

Nancy waited, as though what she'd said was reasonable.

When Carol didn't say anything, Nancy opened the car door and began rifling through their bags.

"I won't take anything that's yours," she said over her shoulder, bundling Carol's still-wet clothes under the seat. Carol knelt down beside her, the gravel crunching into her knees. She tried to stuff Nancy's things back in the bags. Nancy pulled her clothes out of Carol's hands and left the back seat littered with everything she was leaving. She pulled Carol up and kissed her ceremonially on both cheeks.

"Please give them the letter when you get back."

Carol stopped at a gas station across the border. Nancy had given her the rest of the cash, and she had just enough money to get home. Then Nancy left.

She'd let her do it. She'd let her go. For years she thought of how she'd let Nancy go, wondered if she could have persuaded her, forced her into the car, found help. It must be her fault. Nancy had vanished, and it was Carol's fault. Her own life became by contrast more settled, more decided, even by the time she reached Toronto. She held tightly to the wheel as she drove.

At the gas station, she read the letter.

I don't expect you to understand why I need to have a different life from anything you could have imagined for me. But I hope you will trust me and know that I have nothing but love for you.

When she got back to Toronto, she kept the letter for three weeks, not knowing how to deliver it. Finally, she knocked on the door, standing there with the letter in her hand, businesslike, her hair cut short. The short hair is part of her more decided life. She finishes her degree, she begins a graduate program, she meets someone who loves her.

"She gave me this to give to you," she said, thrusting it at Ellen before slouching back down the street in a leather jacket, a show of what looked to Ellen like terrible callousness, as though Carol thought they did not need or deserve compassion.

I have nothing but love for you.

In the old house, Nancy, renamed Naomi, soon finds herself pregnant. This is not entirely surprising; the new world must be peopled. But she had not fully absorbed the possibility of an actual child, she now realizes as she looks at the untroubled waters of the toilet, praying privately for blood after three months of nothing.

John loves her. They sit up together late at night. He has read everything and wants to talk about everything, he pulls books down from the shelves to show her, their heads bent together, his marked passages. His other followers are content to hear him speak, and want only to know what he thinks. Naomi wants to read everything, and have everything connect to everything else, all tending to a single point of incandescence.

Mattie loves her, his face unguarded as a child's at the sight of her. She looks at herself in the speckled mirror, her body fuller, which she'd noticed before but thought a manifestation of satisfaction, that she was replete with conversation and sex, not this inexorable growth.

For weeks she says nothing to anyone. She believes herself selfish, thinking she should be grateful, ready to bestow this gift on Mattie, on John. John speaks very often of gifts that people bestow on each other, and she understands that women, particularly, bestow gifts. She is trying to figure out what it means to be a woman, to be softer and harder, to know when it is proper to have strength and when it is proper to yield. She thinks wildly of her parents. She thinks of arrangements, of doctors they would find for her, of straightened coat hangers.

None of these thoughts are pursued very far (she does not really want to leave), but she secretly has them. *What's a nice middle-class girl like you doing here, darlin'?* Charlie asks her nastily one night, secure in the impeccable misery of his own origins. She considers this, frowning at the line of trees.

She tells John first. He kisses the palms of her hands. Gathers everyone in the living room and makes Mattie kneel. John puts his hands on her still-flat belly and tells her that the baby is a girl. Later, she tells her daughter this story, and still later, she lifts her into a car as she sleeps and leaves in the middle of the night. The girl, waking, twists in her seat and watches her home disappear.

Naomi never tells anyone about doctors or coat hangers. She's chosen this, or been chosen. It doesn't matter now which is which, or whether she can tell the difference.

There are too many people in the house. Mattie has strung a sheet across the middle of the room they sleep in, and Sarah, the girl with the brown braids, sleeps with Charlie on the other side of it; they sometimes call rude things over the curtain. Sarah is pregnant too. Naomi can't sleep and stares at the ceiling. The windows are open and moths, drawn to the light she has switched back on, flicker against the walls, which she's painted yellow, the ceiling blue, anodyne as an imaginary beach. Mattie lies beside her, incredulous at his good fortune. He tells her, haltingly and at her urging, how when he was seven his drunk father cut off his fingertip, then made him tell the doctor he had done it himself, a stupid kid playing with a knife, how Charlie had promised to kill his father for him when they were grown up. Naomi holds him in her arms, mortified by her own childhood. She will, by love, make up for everything. The hubris of that thought does not strike her yet. It does later, when she finds that love does not make up for everything, at least not for Mattie, who left.

She writes Carol a short note requesting a few things. A month later, a box arrives on the porch, addressed in Carol's handwriting but with nothing inside except what she's asked for. No note, no acknowledgement. A few books. Some clothes. Two photographs from her room. Carol and Nancy, standing on the porch, eyes narrowed at the sun. Her parents, on the steps of City Hall in their cursory wedding clothes, her father wearing a suit exactly like all his other suits, her mother in a rumpled dress and tilted hat. Both smiling nimbly into the future that will open into, though they could not have imagined it, this: their daughter, renamed, negligently wrapped in a bedsheet, hauling the box inside. *Into the dangerous world I leapt.*

Doc

HE LAY BACK IN THE WATER. I HELD ONE HAND UNDER his head. He knew he could trust me. The corner of his mouth moved. I thought he was going to say something to me, anything at all, but nothing came. He slipped down in the tub, giving me his weight, crooking up his knees to make room for the rest of him. His knees stuck up, knobby. His head was heavy in my hand.

I was crouched alongside him, in the space between the tub and the wall, kneeling on a mangy towel. Mould bloomed up the tile beside me, a dark candied orange, childhood's hard lumps eye-level on corner store metal shelves. It crumbled when I touched it. I rinsed my hand in the tub, the orange granules mixing with the scum. He turned his head slightly to the left, letting the water rise to his closed eye. The water lapped at the corner of his mouth, but he kept his lips pressed tight, not ready yet. I looked at him upside down. Hollow cheeks, the double scars on each that he insisted came from a knife fight. Seen from this angle I guessed he'd cut himself, alone and looking in the mirror, the world not supplying a fight when he needed one.

I thought he was asleep, but he shifted his head, opened his eyes. Looked up at me like he was trying to think of a joke.

"You okay, Smudge?"

"Yeah."

"Good."

I watched the ripples he'd made by moving, breaking against the sides of the tub like the ripples in the pool stirred up by the wind. He let his head grow heavy in my hand again, closed his eyes. That was the only thing he wanted to say. The water slowly calmed. His breathing slowed. I shifted so I could put both hands behind his head now, lacing my fingers together, so he would feel how securely he was held. I could hear the clock in the hall, which was off by several hours but still ticking. Everything else seemed to grow silent. Him, me, the house, the land around us.

I watched his hand. When he was really passed out, he would twitch his left hand; I'd learned to wait for it. When he'd finally flop down on the couch or fall into his bed, I'd know by his hand twitching that he wouldn't wake again, and both of us were safe for the night.

When his hand twitched, I would let him go.

Later, I tried to explain to my brother about sitting beside Doc, waiting for that final twitch that meant he was asleep, as though he was my child. And he was, really, my first child. I had my own children, eventually. None of them were anything like him.

He once told me the songs used to come to him from else-where, that he'd hear them in the air around him, and he looked

startled, telling me that, more surprised than I was that anything so perfect could come to someone like him.

His hand twitched.

I unlaced my fingers, withdrew my left hand. Let his head
sink lower in the warm water. He didn't move. I worked my
right hand towards the crown of his head, inch by inch, until
the only thing keeping him above the water was the tips of
my fingers. He didn't move. I wanted to kiss his forehead just
before I let go but I thought that might disturb him. He was
so near rest.

I let go.

When my brother asked me for help, I was living in a boarding
house. I had a typewriter, a desk, and a turntable, a mattress
pushed against one wall. The walls were burnt orange and
the brown carpet looked burned too. The sunlight snickered
through metal blinds in the hot wind. When I woke in the
afternoons, the glass of water beside me was always warm. I
kept myself awake at night with diet pills, writing poetry, a
cigarette dangling from my lip. I thought I had to write at
night, that the street outside might offer inspiration, that I'd
know inspiration when I saw it. The part of me with a sense of
humour was embarrassed as I curved over the keys, clacking
out words so loudly that the old man in the room beside mine
once threw his ashtray at our shared wall. I was twenty-three
and called myself a writer after reading in a book that I must
begin to insist I was a writer rather than hoping to be one. All

the writers I loved were dead. I knew no one in the city, except my brother, who paid for the room.

The street was uneventful. At night the noises were disappointingly domestic: a dog barking, a car backfiring, two people arguing on the sidewalk, not loudly enough to qualify as a fight. I was beginning to feel cheated by this utilitarian boulevard, lined with repair shops and second-hand stores, and wasn't curious enough to notice that the hum of the street around me was life, the street and the low-rises and the cleaning women waiting for the bus and the barking dogs as much life as I would ever need or could expect. My poems were loose, unspooling, and about myself.

My brother Graham stood in the doorway of my room, sniffing. We were half-brothers, fifteen years between us; the chest hair that curled over the top button of his shirt was greying. From my spot on the mattress I could see up his nose. I thought of him standing in front of the big mirror in his bedroom, teasing that little tuft around the top button, fretting over the fit of his jeans, trying to look like a man who worked in a music store that sold porn under the counter, not like a music producer with a wife and children and a secret boyfriend only I knew about. I loved my brother even though he was full of shit. He's dead now too.

"I need you to go to Texas. I need you to take care of someone."

The pills had given me a liberating ability to leap to conclusions and I imagined myself following a man into some Houston alley after picking up a gun in a paper bag at a gas station. It would flash from under my coat and I'd never see his face, I'd turn away as he fell, the gun flung into a sewer. None of it made sense, but we'd been raised in northern Alberta by a father who believed certain things were essential for boys, and though we had not met his expectations in any other way, we both knew how to shoot.

"What's funny?" Graham asked, settling himself cautiously on the edge of my mattress.

He didn't mean anything to do with guns. He wanted me to save Doc Sinclair. He thought the world needed Doc, even if Doc threw chairs and couldn't stand up half the time. My brother's particular guilty secret (other than the boyfriend, who really did work in a music store) was that he was not interested in anything other than music, but because it was 1973 he had to pretend to love all the crap around it. He'd stand dourly at a party, staring at the songwriters and resenting how they wasted their time and their energy, the minutes they weren't spending sitting alone, writing songs. He was a puritan; it never occurred to him that some people, like Doc, needed to dull their own edges in order to make anything at all. Graham was simple. All he wanted was to keep the music coming. He tried to impress on me how important this was, with the single-mindedness of a missionary planning the distribution of bibles. It couldn't have been about the money. Doc was such a mess by then that he only played dive bars, forgot his own lyrics, leapt off the stage to fight hecklers. The money came from other singers covering him, adding trills and accompaniments that Doc would have hated if he'd been paying attention. His ballad about bandits had been covered seven times. His death, if anything, would have helped sales while putting an end to embarrassments that were becoming more and more common. But Graham had faith. He thought Doc just needed a little help.

I took a cab from the Houston airport. Graham had given me an envelope with five hundred dollars in it and told me to keep it strapped to my waist even and especially when I went to bed. He'd let Doc know I was coming. Doc hadn't responded.

The old driver smoked enviably, the ash lengthening without falling, and I couldn't figure out how he did it. He was not interested in why I was going so far, except to demand a flat rate that was likely more than letting the meter run. It was evening. I wasn't in a position to argue. Anyway, it wasn't my money.

We left the city behind. The sky we were driving into boiled around the setting sun. As it grew dark, the landscape filled me with dread, and even the brightness of the moon only drew attention to the bareness around us. The road turned to dirt, and there were no lights, only a few houses here and there, the driver cursing softly at the small pings of stones thrown up onto the hood.

The house was unlit. I'd anticipated a shack fallen in on itself, dead vines over the porch. This was a bungalow that looked like it could have been transplanted from a bedroom community in New Jersey. A pool, away to the right, glistened with a scum of rotting leaves. The wind touched the water, shifted the surface.

"This it?" the driver asked, looking up from counting the money I'd handed him. I turned from the shut door, kicking my suitcase over.

"I think so," I said.

He drove off.

I knocked.

I knocked again.

I sat down on my suitcase. I thought I heard a noise behind me, but it was a bat, swooping low over the pool. The wind picked up and the water rippled. I tried to remember how far it was to the last house I'd seen. I took out a bag of chips and my water bottle, resolving to treat the wrenching in my stomach as hunger and not premonition.

The door opened behind me and I spat. I was so sure I would see the figure from the album covers that it took me a moment to comprehend a woman, gaunt and young, unexpected roll of belly over her belt. She flicked the switch beside her. Her hair shone flatly in the light.

"Yeah?"

"I'm Graham's brother."

She drummed her fingers against the doorway, eyes half-shut. "Does Doc know you?"

"He's expecting me."

She closed the door.

I tried to see down the road, looking for a light, wondering how long I could walk.

"He said you can come in."

I followed her down the hall. She dragged one hand reluctantly along the wall behind her.

"Don't bug him, he's tired," she said, pointing at a door to the left. She was older than I'd thought, seen under the hallway's naked bulb. I pushed open the door; behind me, I could hear her leaving the house. I never saw her again.

I was in the living room, which smelled of mildew. He was sitting very straight on a wooden chair, facing a window that looked out onto pockmarked scrub. I felt for a light. He grimaced. He was skinny and regal, a deposed king who refused to acknowledge his fall. He batted his hand down, and I switched the light off again, moved between him and the window. I had a feeling I shouldn't be the first to speak, that I couldn't risk offending him, and that in that moment almost anything could offend him. I wished I had never come.

"Hi, Graham's brother," he said finally.

I told him my name.

"I'll call you Smudge," he said.

"Why?"

He shrugged, staring at me with the same indifference he'd given the view out the window. It didn't matter what was in front of him. He was somewhere else.

"It came to me. Does Graham call you that?"

"Not that I know of."

"I thought he did. I've got a good memory for stuff like that. What does he call you?"

"My name."

"Okay, Smudge."

I smiled slowly, which was something people seemed to like.

"What? What's funny?"

"Nothing."

"Have a seat, Smudge."

He waved a hand at the air in front of him. There was nowhere to sit unless I moved behind him, so I sat down on the floor.

"Great. Another fucking disciple."

"Do you have a lot of disciples?"

"They come and go."

He got up unsteadily, his hands held out, ready to fall. I stayed on the ground, not wanting to make things worse by trying to help. He blundered against another chair that was between him and the door, and I wondered if he'd made himself a track of things that he could grasp when he couldn't get his balance. He found the door frame, leaned against it.

"Good night, Smudge."

He shut the door behind him, and I saw the hall light go off under it, then heard a crash as if he'd fallen against the wall. Then another door closing. Then nothing.

Clouds rolled over the moon. I felt my way to the couch and hoped the squeaking I heard was old springs. The polyester was oily under my hands. I settled myself with my jacket over me. When the moon came out again, I saw a desk with a broken leg, some chairs grouped in a half-circle, his chair by the far window, and a rolled-up carpet, the source of the mildew smell. A collection of bottles lined the wall, which fit what I'd been expecting, except that from the shape I could tell most of them were ketchup. Something scuttled across the floor, and I could hear, so faint I first thought it was coming from outside, a whistling snore. I lay awake, wishing for hostility I could win over, not this high-handed dismissal.

I'd spent the last month listening to his albums and absorbing my brother's anxious reciting of Doc's list: all forms of alcohol except beer because he hated the smell, the same diet pills I took, some others I didn't, pills I'd never heard of.

Doc's songs were about train tracks, whores, border towns, about ghosts in the mountains, about coming home and the death of mothers. He had a voice like a man who'd spent the night crying and then driven a nail into his thumb, who'd grown up in a shanty in the woods next to a still, who knew how to cook squirrels.

None of that was true. He came from New England old money. In the photographs his mother showed me after Doc's funeral, he stood at the edge of the frame, as far as he could get from the other students at the private school that eventually expelled him. His face was soft, bewildered, as if his rage surprised no one more than himself. He broke furniture, set fires, kept knives in boots and under pillows. He did not seem to know how to hold his mouth. The genial snarl that showed his rotten teeth came to him later on. I'd seen it on each album cover. By the last one, five years before he died, he seemed almost at ease, as if he was learning to inhabit himself at last.

The boy with his classmates does not smile, or look directly at the camera, the school uniform fitting badly as though everyone knew he wouldn't stay long. Doc (I can't think of him as James, it so obviously isn't his name, even then) appears slightly out of focus; I like to think his strength of will was strong enough to distort the picture.

"Do you want that one?" his mother asked, sliding it out.

"Oh, no, no."

"Take it."

"I couldn't."

"Take it."

She left it in my hand, my fingers damp on the corners, looking into Doc's averted eyes. She moved off, heels clicking over the murmur of the guests. She had not spoken to him in years. I don't know if anyone in his family had heard a single one of his songs. Sometimes you have to cut your losses.

He would have hated the women with little shreds of black netting over their faces, the minister intoning *whoever has faith in me shall have life even though he die*, and me, standing at the back. He'd have wanted someone to stand apart, incongruous. His three younger brothers, bulky in their dark suits, wore expressions of appropriate masculine grief, but I suspected they were laying their childhood demon to rest. As the coffin was lowered, the youngest brother's mouth twitched involuntarily, and in my mind, continuing the spasm of his lip, he leaned over and spat into the grave.

Doc might have liked that, actually. More like the funeral he would have wanted: an irregular hole in the ground, within sight of a water tower. Night. A little knot of drunks, pouring tequila onto his pine box, the earth kicked over him, maybe a few jagged pieces of concrete stolen from a construction site piled on to keep away coyotes.

When I woke up, it was morning. A headache sliced above my left ear. I went out into the hall. To my left was the open door to the kitchen, and opposite me, two closed doors. I tapped on the nearer one. Listened. There was nothing. I eased the door open.

There were two mattresses under the window, one on top of the other. A blue sleeping bag with feathers sprouting at the seams. No sheets or pillow. Two guitars, propped on their stands, faced each other from opposite corners. The only other furniture was a folding table with a crate pushed under it. No curtains on the window. The moon would shine over him, the sun wake him. Looking back over my shoulder to make sure he wouldn't appear in the doorway, I went to the table, which was empty except for three stacks of index cards, sorted by colour.

I picked up the yellow ones, flipped through. This is it, I thought. This is it.

Man and railroad

He shoots the dog

She can't get a job. There isn't any job

He comes home again because nobody wants his songs but the mine is closed down

Her father dies before she can tell him. Or he dies because she tells him?

In the ditch. The water flows around him. The ditch fills up. It turns into a river.

She finds him. He pours gas around the house. Lights a match while she's sleeping.

A pencil rested beside the cards. It was carefully sharpened, and there were shavings scattered on the floor, but the table was clean.

I read through the cards again. Something was missing—in the cards, in the cleanliness of the table. What I'd loved, listening to his music, was the sense of something beyond the subject of the song that moved underneath it, like the water moving under the wind. Something extra, that was strange and unexplainable and could not be summarized. His voices, I guess.

What was written on the cards was flat, the way the bareness of the room was flat. I'd hoped for crazed visions, a sense I was at the site of a barely contained explosion. I was disappointed. The room felt hollow, which made sense later. It wasn't a room where his voices came to him. It was a room he kept ready in case they ever came back.

I went into the kitchen. A dried cockroach crackled under my bare foot. There was a bowl of old cereal on the table, the milk thin and yellow with floating white globules like dividing cells. I picked up a pot from the stove: canned ravioli burned to the bottom. Beside the counter two fridges stood side by side, half blocking the window. I opened both. Only one was plugged in, and there was nothing in it except liquefying lettuce and a plate with half an onion on it. The other fridge was warm and dry, lined neatly as a doctor's shelf with bottles of pills, white paper bags with prescription labels stapled to the fold.

I opened the cupboards above the counter, lined with stacked matching plates and cups, each white with a brown stripe around the rim. In the lower cupboards I found a stash of cans and a couple of boxes of cereal, which rustled with retreating creatures when I touched them.

"If you want something to eat, open a can. We're out of milk," he called from the side door.

I hadn't heard him come in. He was standing with a broom in one hand, the bristles plastered with wet leaves.

"I thought I'd clean the pool," he said, leaning the broom against the counter.

I looked out the window. He'd given up fast. I turned back to the cans, wondering if mushroom soup or beef stew were feasible this early in the morning. He shambled past to the living room door.

"Hang on, did you sleep on the couch?"

"Where was I supposed to sleep?"

I thought he was mocking me, but when I looked over, he was grinning shamefacedly, genuinely sorry.

"Shit, man. I figured Arlene would show you. What a bitch. Come here."

I followed him into the hall, where he leaned against the wall, pointing at the door to the right of his.

"I thought it was a bathroom."

"Nope. That's through the kitchen. Did you like my song cards?"

"I—"

"Saw you through the window."

"I didn't mean to—"

"Don't worry about it. What's mine is yours and what's yours is mine."

He clapped me on the shoulder. I could smell his breath, the ruin of his teeth between the gold caps. But he didn't frighten me in the light. He was shorter, about my height, scrawny, with exhausted green eyes. Friendly. Harmless.

The room was square, the floor swept, a dark patch of hair and dirt left in one corner. A mattress, made up with yellow flowered sheets. A brown pressboard dresser with brass handles, the top blistered and peeling, and the bottom drawer missing. I lifted my suitcase onto it. The sheets looked fresh, the dresser had been wiped. Care had been taken.

"Okay, just so I don't get mad about you snooping, I need you to run an errand for me. Why don't you go buy us some groceries? Like, real bread and eggs and coffee? Then you can get some J&B while you're at it. Or maybe bourbon. Both?"

His tone was wheedling. I didn't answer.

"Come on, Smudge. We can get a good big breakfast in."

"I can't."

He folded himself down onto the mattress. Offered the spot beside him. I stayed standing, thinking of Graham.

"Now, Smudge. You're here to look after me, right?"

I nodded.

"That cocksucker brother of yours, he's a good guy, I love that guy, he's been a real friend to me, but you agree he's in way over his head. You know. Yeah. I thought you would. So, you can run me a couple of errands when I need, and I won't be stupid, I won't, you know, *overdo it*, I'll be smart and stick to plain whiskey for a while, and maybe some codeine because of that song I wrote, and Graham's happy. And I'm happy. And you too, I guess, whatever makes you happy."

He winked at me. His voice was sharper, sober, the New England private school boy showing through underneath the drawl, like an erased drawing still visible in the pressure of the pencil. It made me feel warmer towards him: we were both performing ourselves, even if his performance was more roomy, more lived-in. That was okay. I'd had less practice.

"I don't have a car."

"Yeah, I know. But I do."

"Okay. Draw me a map."

He stood up. Stretched his arms over his head, smiling at his success.

"Good boy, Smudge."

When I came back, he was playing in his room, sitting on the crate. I left the bags on the table and stood in the doorway, watching him.

He stopped, listening to the notes die away, began again, repeating the same phrase over and over, not able to get beyond it. He shook his head at himself, muttered. Tried again. Again. Cursed softly. Stopped again, listening, and he kept on listening even when the strings had stopped vibrating, as if there might be something there, in the silence. He growled, a low warning sound, not meant for me. A string of words under his breath, too rapid for song, as if he was furiously discarding in hopes of finding the right word somewhere in the piled chaff of his mind. He shook his head again. Began again.

He didn't turn, but he knew I was there, though I think he wanted me to believe he didn't know.

When he was playing, everything about him had a purpose. Every clench and tremor, latently violent or just pathetic the minute he stopped, was caught up. Patches of sweat under his arms, along his back, the dirty T-shirt stuck to him. He rocked prayerfully back and forth, ground out his half words, his right foot arched up on the heel like he would tap time, but he kept it raised, as if maintaining tension was the only hope he had for finding the song.

Every time he started playing, I saw the desperate hope in him, that this time he would find it. There were even times when he seemed near, when something wilder or sweeter came into his voice and the sound of the guitar, but then he pressed too hard and it was gone.

I watched him until he stopped trying. Laid the guitar down on the floor. Nudged it with his foot like he wanted to kick it across the room but didn't have the strength.

By evening, he was so drunk he couldn't talk. I laid him on his side and went to bed.

We went on that way for a while. I fed him and myself. I cleaned, a little. Just the kitchen, not the pool or the yard. He didn't even clean his body. I grew used to the smell of him. He ate less than I did, and we both ate like five-year-olds: eggs and bread, canned soup, packages of red licorice he opened with his teeth, spitting the cellophane onto the floor for me to pick up when I felt like it. The cockroaches retreated in the daylight, which seemed like a working compromise, as much as the drinks I allowed him, rationing them out while he played, then letting him have a full bottle and whatever pills he needed to get to sleep. I didn't lie to my brother; I didn't tell him anything at all. There was no phone. Once, he sent a postcard: *Anything you need? Money,* I wrote back, with Doc chuckling in the background, and it came, by courier.

He always played with his back to me, facing the empty room, and I watched the bare skin of his neck as he bent his head. As the days became weeks and months, I thought, now he'll turn around, now he'll ask me to face him, but it never happened. I just watched the back of his neck. The skin pale because his hair usually covered it, the tracing of scratches, broken capillaries. If love is the absence of fear, he loved me then in the way he allowed me to see the gaps where he stopped playing, listening for what he wished would arrive, what never arrived. He let me see the doubt in his silence. The tension of his bent head reminded me of a small boy hiding, listening for approaching footsteps. Wanting to be found. Waiting, beginning to be afraid that no one is coming. No one is coming ever again. I'd see that fear in his face, and it was the bottomless terror of a child who knows, suddenly and with certainty, that there is no help. The person who called his ex-wives rancid cunts and coughed phlegm into the pool, the one against whom I locked my door at night, that person, briefly, ceased.

He shouldn't have trusted me.

Though maybe he knew that. I think he knew that.

Or maybe he should have trusted me. I gave him what he wanted.

On bad nights, he broke things. I bought myself a deadbolt, after a night spent staring at the flimsy lock on my bedroom door. In the morning, there was glass everywhere. He was always sorry and never said so, sauntering out the door to stare at the pool. I think he was disappointed in me, hoping I would follow him out, push him to a fight. Instead, I got the broom. I bought new glasses, then Mason jars, which held more whiskey and shattered less easily.

Every day, usually in the lull of the first drink after breakfast, he'd stand by the pool. The wet leaves gleamed in the morning sun. Sometimes he'd kneel, dip in his hand, stirring to make an eddy. Watch the smaller ripples from the wind, when there was a wind. He was fascinated as a cat, and it kept me from cleaning out the pool. I thought the marshy smell would keep him from going in, that revulsion would override the wish to have the water close over his head.

"This is it," he said one night, still without turning.

I didn't answer, not sure if we still kept the conceit that I wasn't really there.

"Did you hear me, Smudge?"

Like he was afraid I'd go too.

"I heard you."

"You and me. This is it."

"Love you too, asshole."

"Don't get sappy, Smudge," his voice terse, saving face, and his head went down again and he kept playing and I waited.

"If I ask you for something, will you say yes?"

"Yes."

"Good boy."

"Can I know what it is?"

His head went down. It's so hard to tell, afterwards, how much you did or didn't know. Sometimes I think I only guessed as I eased my hand out from under his head, and I even think I may have been wrong and made the wrong guess, but then I feel the weight of his head again, the weight of his relief and his sleep, the way his hand twitched, and I am certain that I did what he wanted. I absolve myself. No one else can.

He didn't look up again. I felt invisible, but I was what he needed: one listener who attempted to love him and sometimes really did love him, and who would say yes when he asked. This is it. This is it.

Unlike me, he never locked his door. That night, I went in. He slept uncovered, his hands under his chin, in a wife beater and boxers. Sleeping, he was beautiful. His pallid filthiness less sordid, more like wax. I sat on the floor beside him, easing myself down so the boards didn't creak.

I will note here, since it's the place to note it, that I have never in my life been sexually interested in other men. This was something purer than that, though pure is the wrong word, I don't mean desire is impure and the way I looked at him (for a long time, not moving) was exalted. I mean more in the other direction. Desire still carries curiosity or recognition that another person exists. I looked at him the way a large animal might look at me, if it found me in the woods, and it was hungry, and I was asleep.

I wanted to understand how he'd made the songs, even if he couldn't make them anymore. Asleep, his defences down, I thought I'd be able to see it. But there was nothing. He was just a thin man who couldn't stay sober. Frail and defeated as an old drunk lying on a bench in the afternoon sun in late fall. He stirred, struggling with a dream. He was the loneliest creature I'd ever seen. I sat, watching him sleep, thinking he'd wake up.

In my memory, I stayed awake the whole night, watching him jealously, but I know I fell asleep beside his bed and woke up and went to my own room just as the sun rose. People only sit up all night like that in songs.

In the morning, he smoked five cigarettes in a row, sipping cough medicine with a Do Not Mix with Alcohol warning on the side. He shook his head at me, looked down at his feet, arching the right as though he was playing.

"Good boy, Smudge," he said again, almost to himself.

He had the upper hand in the bargain between us because I've spent the rest of my life not knowing if I did right. I was his dupe. He loved deals with the Devil stories, which can only go one way: the man believes he can get the best of the Devil until the day the debt is called in. He even had a song about that, "Man at the Crossroads." You've probably heard it somewhere. It was pretty famous, for a while. Dylan even did a version during his fundamentalist phase. But it wasn't really a religious song. Doc didn't believe in God. Just in the Devil, lounging at the crossroads, playing with a set of cards. It's a great song. I hear it fairly often in cafés. He's having one of his upswings again. I wish my brother could be around to know it.

I went with my brother to the funeral. He lent me a suit. We didn't talk much on the flight to Boston, both of us thinking of everything ahead. My brother was his executor, and dealt with the inquest, trying to hurry everything for the sake of Doc's family, who were desperate to bury him. None of his ex-wives answered our calls. I didn't blame them. They'd fled like you'd run from a burning house. As the plane touched down, he patted my arm clumsily, his eyes on the large hair of the woman in front of him.

"I don't blame you."

"Thanks."

"You did everything you could."

I didn't know if that was true. I didn't know if Graham thought it was true.

I heard Doc playing in his room. He hummed jerkily, like someone with a stammer trying to get out an obstinate word. I looked at the back of his neck. The lank hair falling to one side to show the skin, grey-white as a skinned fish, reddened with long scratches. He put the guitar down, jerked his bare foot, and sent it skidding hard against the table.

"Come on, Smudge," Doc said, getting up. "Time for a bath."

Householders

NAOMI WAS TALKING TO HERSELF, WALKING ALONG Bloor near St. George on a windy day, listing slightly towards the high red wall beside her. Justifications, protestations. She had taken to walking alone, to get away from her parents and her daughter. She'd run away, with Trout, from the commune in Maine where Trout had been born, and they were staying in her parents' house. They had no money and nowhere else to go. She had not seen or spoken to her parents in more than ten years, and they must have often thought her dead.

She walked to get to know the city again, but talking to herself so enclosed her in her own thoughts that she barely knew where she was. She realized she must look like the women she noticed sometimes on the street, just maintaining their hold, lips moving, making their way through crowds that instinctively parted for them. She had seen that circumspect look on the faces of strangers whose eyes she'd accidentally caught. She must smell of ruin. The barely discernible tinge of something beginning to burn.

She happened to lift her eyes and saw Carol running past, dodging the scudding newspapers, carrying, as in her memory, a bag that looked heavy with books, though the bag was now burnished leather with a brass clasp. Naomi had not tried to find her. She was about to keep going when Carol turned, her long grey professorial coat filling like a sail.

"Nancy? Oh my God! Nancy."

"It's me," Naomi said, feeling younger, exposed. Wanting to stand on one foot or put her hands behind her back.

"Nancy. I thought I'd never see you again."

Naomi didn't know what to say to that except, rudely, "Well, you are seeing me."

Carol dropped her bag on the sidewalk and hugged her. She had an astringent smell, not the sandalwood soap Naomi remembered. Carol's hands were trembling.

Carol's hair was short, sandy with some white threads, and her face was a little fuller, with lines around her eyes and mouth. Her eyelids were peacock green. She wore tapered black trousers, showing under the hem of her coat, heavy silver jewellery looped around her throat and wrists, and a man's watch, perhaps her father's. Naomi had liked Carol's father the few times she'd met him, and wondered if he was dead, and was sorry. Carol smiled uncertainly, waited for her to smile back. Naomi's lips scraped over her teeth, but she achieved the desired effect. She patted the front of her skirt, conscious of the layers of sweater, her friend Sarah's old boots that she'd stolen when she left.

"I have to dress up for work," Carol said, misunderstanding, her hand worrying at the collar of her white shirt. Naomi almost expected her to pick up her bag and rush off. Instead she hugged Naomi again, more forcefully, and took her to Dooney's, where she bought her a coffee and a slice of dense cheesecake, which Naomi picked apart with her fork.

Carol eased out of her coat. In the past, she would have been direct, demanding that Naomi give an account of herself, acquiesce to Carol's sense of her failures. All the things Carol had needed, reassurance, acknowledgement, praise. People on the outside needed that. Naomi had been warned about the outside. She'd left anyway. She looked out the window, clouded by steam.

Carol went on with her adjustments, pushing the bracelets up and down her wrist, buttoning her shirt cuff and then unbuttoning it. Pulling a flop of hair to one side over her forehead. She smiled again. Her teeth were very white. Naomi's were yellow, her cheeks sunken from several missing molars. Carol kept twisting in the chair. How women fussed. How they preened and fidgeted. Naomi sat severely, her hands folded in her lap.

"Nancy—"

"That's not my name anymore. Remember. I said in the note I sent. I'm Naomi now."

"I don't know if I can call you that."

"It's my name."

She spoke without anger, watching Carol's face.

"Not for me."

"John gave it to me when he blessed me."

John's name was strange in her mouth; she hadn't talked much about him to her parents. That part of her life was mystifying to them. She was not sure she would ever be able to explain, to her parents or to Carol if she asked.

"John that old man?"

"He was my teacher."

Carol gave in showily, holding up her hands. "Okay. Naomi."

A silence. She was afraid that Carol might cry.

"You disappeared."

"To you."

"I kept that note for years. I kept thinking I should try to find you. I threw it out last year when we moved. You were pregnant and you needed more clothes. Then nothing."

"Trout. She's ten."

"Like the fish?"

"John gave the name to her."

Silence again. She saw Carol make herself ask.

"And the man, the father?"

"Mattie."

"Right. Mattie. You said when you wrote."

"Oh, he left. When she was a baby. Just after we got settled on the land."

They both sat, thinking of Mattie with his feckless smile, whom Naomi could see in her daughter's face and who for Carol was barely even a memory.

"Where were you?" Carol asked finally.

"In Maine. We bought land there. Near a smaller town. We called it—John called it—the Other Kingdom."

"*Those who have crossed/With direct eyes, to death's other kingdom?*"

"Yes."

"Huh."

"No, it made sense. If you were there."

A pause.

"So what the hell are you doing here, then?"

Carol meant to keep her tone light but Naomi drew back, setting down the fork.

"I left in the night. I stole a car. With Trout."

"Holy shit."

"I wasn't strong enough to stay."

"That's ridiculous."

Naomi did not bother with politeness. She was out of the habit, anyway. Politeness was not a virtue where she had lived. "You have no idea what you're talking about."

"How on earth would I know what I was talking about?" Carol asked, fully serious now.

Silence. There was no answer to the truth of that.

"Where are you living?" Carol asked briskly, determined to bring the conversation under control.

"With my parents. I need to get work and somewhere to live. We can't stay there. They don't—they have no idea what to do with me."

"Did they ever?" Carol asked, making a face.

They laughed, relieved to be able to laugh.

"What do you do?" Naomi asked, glancing at the leather bag, submitting to what she hoped Carol wanted.

"I teach. Women's Studies, U of T. Hence the getup. Like David Bowie, Laura says. She might be trying to be kind."

Naomi looked blank.

"You know nothing about me."

Naomi thought she'd been about to say "You know nothing" but had saved herself in time. They looked at each other, and whatever resolution Carol had made faltered.

"I thought you were dead. I thought I killed you, leaving you there."

Naomi again hoped Carol wouldn't cry.

"I could have asked your parents, of course, phoned them. I could have. I run into your mother sometimes, or I see her anyway, you know, walking somewhere. But how do you ask that? Nancy—did she die? People did. Some of them. People we knew."

Naomi did not ask which people, as Carol expected her to.

"You look just the same to me," Carol said, very quietly.

"I'm not the same."

"I didn't say that."

"I'm *not* the same."

Carol reached across the table and Naomi thought she was going to touch her, but she forked up the crumbles of cheesecake instead.

"If you won't eat it, I will."

Carol finished the cake and went on talking. Naomi pulled at the end of her braid.

Sometimes, when Carol paused, Naomi saw her eyeing the braid, perhaps thinking of Naomi in the old house they'd shared as students, leaning over the sink, her washed hair dripping on the grey floor. Carol recovered herself, continued to fill Naomi in on more than ten years of missed life.

Naomi looked around her, at the terracotta tiles, the coffee machine, the plate-laden waitress deftly balanced, and could not find a way to convey to Carol how impossible that task was.

She had no way to understand her surroundings yet; everything was frantic and unheeding. How little she knew. In the Other Kingdom she'd known everything. She was brow-beaten by the profusion of detail here, and how the details seemed to add up to not very much, how an attitude of feverish competence was mistaken for a life. Details would not clarify anything.

Details bewildered her, but they were what Carol offered. The mechanics of teaching, departmental politics, the woman, Laura, with whom she lived (she said this defiantly; Naomi kept her expression unreadable), the house they had bought and whether they had paid too much for it, how this or that neighbourhood had changed, how Carol herself had changed her views on something they had once agreed on or something they had once argued over. Naomi could not have accounted for her life in that way. All she could think when Carol asked her questions was that she had sinned, in a number of ways, against herself and against her child, but a word like *sin* would have been meaningless to Carol, with her talk of political consciousness, of rights. Part of Naomi's delusion, her belief in irrevocable gestures. Naomi felt an antipathy so strong she almost got out of her chair. There was nothing she could say to this glossy woman, possessed of such assured resentments.

Carol stopped talking, hesitated, then leaned over the table and covered Naomi's hands with her own.

"I'm sorry. I'm talking too much."

Naomi shook her head, ashamed of her thoughts.

"I find it very difficult to see you," Carol said, stricken. "Can I say that? I find it difficult." She got up. "Will you come to my house?"

"What?"

"I'm having a dinner party next week."

"A party?"

Carol smiled. "Not a *party*. Just a dinner. A few people. Good people."

Naomi gestured at herself. "I'm not really an ideal dinner party guest."

"I'd like to see you in my house."

Naomi must owe this to Carol. She believed she could see Carol thinking this.

"Please come."

"Okay. You win. I'll come."

Carol made Naomi write her number in a small red notebook, wrote her own along with an address and date and time on a torn-out page, which she folded and pressed down on the table. She kissed Naomi's cheek, touched her braid. Her fingers were manicured, softened. Naomi watched her stride to the door, regaining her authority, her ease in herself as she moved, her legs wide as a sailor's. She shouldered the door open and was gone in a rush of cold air.

The waitress came to clear the empty plate.

"I'll sit here, thanks," Naomi said, picking up the cooled coffee.

"Great," the waitress answered tonelessly, turning away.

If she had stayed in Toronto like Carol and been more like Carol or who Carol now appeared to be, she might have sat here often, she thought. She looked at the women at other tables, women ruefully approaching the middle of their lives (she had not thought much about aging, but there were mirrors here, more faces to compare to her own, store windows in which to catch sight of herself). These were probably women who could give an account of themselves, or at least more of an account than she could. Some list of purchases and losses, newspaper subscriptions and thoughts on elections at home and abroad, a working knowledge of scandals, perhaps they fretted over the question of the right school for their children, a school that would confirm their children in what they themselves believed. I followed an old man into the woods, she thought, and tried to live a right life. She laughed silently at herself and the other people at the tables until she found she was crying instead, and had to go out into the street before anyone noticed, turning off Bloor and down Brunswick, where there were fewer people.

Toronto was foreign. She wondered if the bookstores on Harbord where she and Carol had browsed as students were still there. A woman passed by, looked away. She turned and watched the woman go, noticing the bulky line of her blazer, the stuffed shoulders. Yuppies, Carol had said, waving her hands at the people they passed as they walked to the restaurant. Naomi didn't know the word, and Carol incredulously explained it. It was obviously an insult, though Naomi couldn't see what distinguished Carol from the people she denigrated. She was so accomplished, so intent. Wasn't that what it meant? And it did not seem possible that such a thorough change had taken place, as though in Naomi's time with Carol everyone had been one thing and now the decade had shifted, everyone, presumably the same people, had become, regrettably or not, another completely different thing, both the present and their memories inhabited by facile definitions rather than actual lives.

The trees looked the same, Naomi thought, walking towards Harbord Street, scraping the back of her hand along the bark of one, hard enough to raise lines on her skin.

Of course she could not tell Carol very much, unable to convey the first thing about how she had lived. Raising a child who had never seen an apartment building, a subway, a TV screen, never sat in a movie theatre, never idly glanced at a watch on her wrist. At first Naomi's father, Harold, had teased Trout, with a serious face, a whisper of pretend horror at her ignorance, but he stopped when he saw how the city filled her with dread. She'd dragged Trout into a place of shunting machines, a place where, hearing someone cry out, you quickened your pace and kept walking. The first time she'd persuaded Trout to go on the subway with her, Trout gripped her arm so hard she thought she'd find a bruise later on. She'd gone with Trout to see her mother's dentist after Ellen had looked in Trout's mouth and hers. They passed a man yelling on a street corner in front of the Baptist church by Dufferin station, calling on God to save all sinners, his clothes too thin for the wind, waving a limp black bible.

"Hurry up," Ellen said. "We'll be late."

But Trout twisted her head, staring at the man, as though, in the whole city, here was someone she recognized.

The night of the dinner party, Naomi put on a bead necklace that she found in the box on her childhood dresser, brushed her hair. She noticed herself in a new way, the way a woman notices herself in the presence of strangers. Noticed that her hands had been made red by scrubbing recalcitrant stains, that the pads of her fingers were beginning to wrinkle, that rough flushed patches sometimes appeared on her neck. Her face was shiny, the tip of her nose faintly pink. She could not bring herself to wear makeup, though it was apparently commonplace. Even Carol, with her metallic eyelids.

"Are you going to wear those horrible boots?" her mother, Ellen, asked from the doorway.

"What else would you suggest?"

"I could lend—"

"I'm not going anywhere in a pair of your pumps."

"You'd break an ankle, you don't know how to wear them. I thought some nice flats."

"A pink cardigan with pearl buttons?"

"You kept that one?" Suppressed vindication in her mother's voice.

"I cut it up for a quilt."

She wished she had not said that. Her mother did not deserve that. Though it had been a good quilt. Trout had loved it, slept under it for years, until it was just a symbolic square laid over more durable blankets, ragged at the edges.

"Well," Ellen said. She held out a box.

"What?"

"Will you just open it?"

Naomi took the box. Heavy earrings in the shape of leaves lay on a puff of cotton, each vein etched along the surface of the silver.

"I bought them, I don't know, five years ago? Three years? I just thought—I thought of you. Where you were. I didn't really know where you were. I hoped you were somewhere. Woods. All I could think was woods."

A warning in her voice, slipping into plaintiveness.

"I don't know if the holes are still there," Naomi said tightly, touching her earlobes.

"What happened to those little gold flowers you had? I looked for them once in your room. Do you still have them?"

"No. I lost them."

She remembered the day they'd been sold, bartering with the man in the car, his wife holding them in her pink palm. She and Sarah, selling clay bells by the roadside, the dust in the summers. Smiling, hoping the cars would stop, the drivers buy bells and whatever else had been scrounged up to sell. Hoping more desperately as time went on. Not enough money, not enough food. Worry and hunger always in her gut.

"Could you try these?" Ellen asked.

One slid in easily, the other resisted. Naomi jabbed the earring hard into the regrown skin. Ellen flinched.

"There. I'm in balance."

"Why are you dressed like that?" Trout asked as Naomi came down the stairs, suspicious of her loose hair and loose skirt and shirt, the leaves swinging from her reddened lobes.

"I'm going to a party."

"Where?"

"An old friend invited me."

"You said we don't have any friends here."

"Someone I knew a long time ago. Before you were born."

The corners of Trout's mouth turned down, not wanting to think before her own birth, all the things she did not know and could not fathom.

"Will you be out when I go to bed?"

"You're too old to think about that," Ellen said. "You're a big girl."

"Can I come with you?"

"No, sweetheart."

"We will have our own party," Harold announced.

"Why can't I come?"

"It's not that kind of party," she said.

She hoped to find Trout in her bed when she came home. Trout would sneak along the hall. Ellen thought there was something uncouth, even morally lax, in children sharing a bed with their parents. Naomi could not sleep without Trout there, her hair plastered to her scalp in the too-hot bedroom. Alone, she lay awake feeling the air rise from the vent underneath the bed. In the farmhouse, she'd been almost tearfully glad in winter for the warmth of her people when it was so cold they dragged bedding down into the front room where the wood stove was.

The hot, dry air made her irritable. How quickly old feelings returned, her pique at less than satisfactory surroundings, as though the world owed her comfort. How quickly she resumed being a person who swore under her breath when objects and circumstances did not obey her. She was forgetting how to be patient. It frightened her.

She knew the walk would be short; she recognized the address as near the house where she'd grown up. Two streets and she was nearly there, wondering what kind of party it was. A party was a fire in the field, children running in and out of the circle of light. She thought of the night they'd moved to their land, arriving in vans and old cars. They'd built a fire and danced around her and Sarah, both pregnant with holy children. Very late, just as the fire was dying, John proclaimed in one of his precipitous revelations that all personal objects from their lives before, photographs, lockets around necks, letters, any private thing, must be thrown in to revive the fire. There was a silence, each person thinking of the few things they'd kept, but Naomi ran to her bag and flung everything that meant her life before into the heart of the blaze. She was glad to. It was right, she knew: she must be free of everything, dizzy with the liberty of all her losses. Her parents' faces blistering in green and blue as the photograph she'd kept melted. Her younger self, standing with Carol on the porch of the house in Toronto, arms comradely around each other's shoulders. Her mother's lace shawl, going up in delicate webs. She smashed her grandmother's teapot against the rocks in the centre of the fire. The pieces turned brown, then black, obliterating the mawkish blue roses. She stood up, clapping her hands, yelling that anyone who wouldn't do the same wasn't ready, and everyone else, rebuked, scrambled to follow her.

She had been mistrustful of happiness, as a demand or even a recognizable state of being. She would kick happiness to pieces, along with every other civilized delusion. Now she remembered happiness as a tangible, even visible thing, something she had in fact possessed. Dwelt in, between the ache and cramp of endless work and, in her pregnancy, throwing up in the bushes and covering the splatter with leaves, not wanting to show weakness. Trout as a small child, waving her hands in the blue evening air. Naomi lying on the ground beside her, watching a storm of songbirds shaking a tree above them, or listening to the river, forwarding on, wearing away the small stones on the bed over a hundred years. Because of John she'd learned to really hear the river and the birds and been part of them, been part of her child hearing those things. Surprised by sacredness, arriving in the middle of the ordinary day. He told her that if she was attuned to the world, she could find union anywhere, as profound as her own birth, or the birth of her daughter, or even her death. She'd believed it. Trout would have an infinite consciousness. It was later that Trout seemed to her bounded and trussed by the smallness of her life: the same faces and thoughts, cold winters, never enough to eat.

She thought of Carol's decorated neck and wrists, pictured canapés, the clink of ice in murder-weapon glasses, too at a loss to grasp at anything beyond the clichés of a housekeeping magazine in the dentist's office when she'd had her rotten teeth pulled.

She looked in the lit windows along Palmerston as she passed. Children sprawled on carpets, men and women setting tables, entire families gathered around the television's flickering green-and-blue eye. There was so little darkness. Even on this tepid street, she could feel the city whirring through her. The narrow brick house, when she reached it, seemed to have light in every room.

She stood on the sidewalk, late but unable to move. She made herself walk up the stairs and ring the bell, which chimed twice.

The door was answered by a woman in the act of saying something over her shoulder.

"Come in. Come in. She's here!" she called, giving Naomi a view of stretched neck.

"Bring her in!" came Carol's voice, with the forced excitement of the hostess. "I've just got my head stuck in the oven."

"I'm Laura," the woman said. "Let me take your coat."

She was very skinny, in a loose black shirt and pants like a person hired to serve drinks. Her hair was dyed dark, lustreless as coal. Thick makeup covered freckles or slightly blemished skin. She was very young. Naomi wondered if she'd been Carol's student. She shook the coat before hanging it, as though expecting a puff of dust, and turned back to Naomi, who was struggling with her laces. Naomi tried to look up in an innocuous, friendly way that showed she was not a pitiable figure.

Carol, oven-mitted, holding a pan of something that steamed up into her face, said, "I know I'm supposed to be a vegetarian, but I just can't do it. I mean, smell that!" as the pan slopped to one side, bubbling gravy around a brown haunch. Seeing Naomi, she dashed it down on the stovetop and gripped her shoulders, still wearing the oven mitts, as Laura handed her a glass of wine without asking.

There were three other people in the kitchen, two women and one man, standing in the corners out of Carol's orbit, their smiles fixed expectantly in a way that made Naomi assume a quick sketch before her arrival of what Carol thought she knew: lost years, a mistaken idealism of the kind that they had all jettisoned in favour of other goods, like this kitchen, while she had soldiered on until she'd hit the wall. What a waste. What a shame.

Carol had already turned back to the stove, leaving her in the silence, which was so far only several seconds but was crossing over into memorable unease.

Only a year ago, she'd stopped at the bar in town, walking in off the street after buying groceries. Used the bathroom, balancing the box on one knee and soaping her hands at length, greedy for the sting of very hot water. The mirror was blotched and distorting, and she did not look at herself. Coming out of the bathroom, she heard Nancy Sinatra insisting *these boots were made for walking*. She remembered that song, remembered herself in school, also named Nancy, wondering if that was what a woman was. Scornful, controlled. It wasn't, not for her, standing on the ground-down carpet among the early drinkers. How far she'd come. She felt magnificent, the box balanced on her sharp hip bone, tramping out the door, back into her life with John's teachings and her companions and her daughter.

These strangers watching her were real now, that other life effaced. She wished Carol had not seen her on the street. She wished she was not here.

She drank, the white wine cool and tingling, her first glass of wine in over ten years. Carol, sloughing off the oven mitts, performed introductions. Annie, Izzy, Robert. Naomi took a tentative second sip.

Annie and Izzy stood slightly turned towards each other. Naomi supposed they must be a couple, getting herself used to the idea, allowing herself to think about it but not too much. Perhaps they were Carol's colleagues. They had the subtly expensive clothes and air of detached self-importance that Naomi associated with academics. Her parents had had it too, she remembered, before she destroyed them, though their satisfaction had been quieter and weightier, in keeping with their generation.

Robert was scruffier than the women, in a pilled sweater and jeans, hole in the red toe of one woolly sock. He said that he'd heard a *lot* about her. He was stooped, with fluffy brown hair to his shoulders, and was rendered piratical by one gold earring. Naomi hoped he was not intended, with Carol's hearty blundering, for her, as though she was in need of a table companion or potential lay (did Carol still say *lay*? did anyone still say *lay*? what did they say? what did she know?).

She whispered to Carol, "I don't eat meat."

"Oh no. Oh no. I should have thought."

"I'll eat salad. I'm not very hungry."

"There's potatoes too. And carrots. I'm a terrible host."

They sat down to dinner, Carol red in the face at her mistake, too talkative because of it. Carol had always needed to do the right thing. Naomi served herself, abstained from a third sip of wine.

"We lived together in this house on Manning," Carol was saying. "It was my first place away from home. God, it was a mess. We thought cleaning was *bourgeois*."

She laughed, at herself and at Naomi. The others joined in the laugh, though not Robert, Naomi saw. He smiled at her as if they might together make Carol the joke.

"Of course, my mother never let me lift a finger," Carol went on. "I was too smart for that, she was scared she would ruin me, typical aspirational Catholic housewife, and Naomi was a princess, she always had cleaning ladies, plus her parents were pretty laid-back about stuff like that. Her mother was the first female professor I ever met. There were other people in the house too, it was one of those turnstile houses. You know how it is, you lose touch. I wasn't out yet, and that can really change how you see yourself. Carrying that around all the time, thinking it's this thing you'll never tell."

Murmurs of assent from the table. Naomi noticed how Carol hit her name hard, trying to grow accustomed to it. How different Carol's memories must be of what she'd done and how she'd left. She wondered now if she'd broken Carol's heart. The thought would not have occurred to her.

"And then Naomi and me went on this road trip, we didn't really know where we were going, we thought we were looking for the revolution, but we did a lot of driving until we ended up in this tiny town in Maine, we were just passing through but we went to hear this old man, I don't know what he called himself, a leader? A healer? He gave a sermon in this house, and we went, and Naomi decided to stay. So I drove back by myself."

Naomi, seized on as a subject for conversation, was persuaded to describe the land, the clay bells, the sermons. She was surprised to find herself so voluble, but she kept on, seeing Carol's face. Naomi owed her this: an explanation, a spectacle. She would be an object of curiosity. Then she abruptly stopped talking, pressed her napkin to her mouth, thinking of Trout as a naked child in the mud by the river as she washed sheets, stooped in the current, the threadbare membrane of cotton spread over the water.

"Wait, wait," Robert said. "The Other Kingdom. I went there for a couple of days. I don't remember the year, maybe '76? '77? To hear him speak. That was you! Maybe we met."

"Those were the good years," Naomi said, "when we thought we were the next phase of the world." She smiled, not enough for her listeners to know if she was serious or not.

Carol scowled, picked a sprig from her tongue.

"I remember looking at the house. I didn't go past the main field, though, I didn't intrude. I mean, you really lived there. I was just a tourist."

"We lost a bunch of our vegetables in the early days when people came to hear him. Stoned kids trampling around in the dark. Only for a few years though, then we went out of fashion."

"Well, it wasn't me. I promise."

"I didn't bear a grudge. We didn't bear grudges."

"He was amazing," Robert went on to the table, his face flushed. "We all had to sit, and he stood on this stump, it was as the sun was rising, you had to get up before the light came and then there was this procession in the dark, and he leapt onto the stump and *preached*, this real preaching as the sun rose. He had everything at his fingertips, the Upanishads, the Bible, half the books I'd ever heard of and a bunch I'd never heard of, he just snatched it up out of the air, and you felt you could know everything, just by hearing him. You lived there. You *lived* there." He stopped talking, looked at Naomi in what appeared to be wonder.

"Yes," Naomi said at last, spearing a radish.

"And did it feel like you knew everything?" he asked urgently.

"Yes!" she said, and gulped from her glass as Carol laughed too loudly, but he was in earnest and so was she.

"I did watch, I guess I did spy," he said, ducking his head as though relieved he had someone to confess to. "I watched where you lived, I hid in the trees for a while, on the second day. I watched you all sitting at that table. Talking to him. And there was this very tall man who made those bells you guys sold. They were beautiful. He was beautiful. He was so focused. I watched him for a long time. You were all really quiet. I envied you. I think I envied you. I was pretty angry then. I was angry at everything. You all looked like you were past that."

"We weren't allowed," Naomi said distinctly, "to show anger. It's not the same as not feeling it."

"Of course," he said, chastened, though she hadn't meant any kind of rebuke. She was moved to think of him among the trees, watching them sitting at the table with their heads bowed, listening to words he couldn't catch, wrapped in a life he was not troubled enough to truly want.

"I got impatient with separatism pretty quickly," Carol said. She'd been drinking steadily. "God knows we tried that, for a while. Go away, stay pure. Go away and mistrust everything. Run away and be some kind of authentic new thing."

"I wasn't, I didn't—" Naomi said, pushing her chair back an inch.

"Maybe it's because I wasn't religious, so it didn't attract me, I mean my parents were, so I'd already worked through that shit," Carol went on, speaking over Naomi. "Having a leader, being a disciple. It just seemed irresponsible, it's not like governments rush to disarm because people meditate on the cosmos, it's not

like some poor fifteen-year-old can get an abortion any easier
if we start making our own clothes and barricade our kids in
the middle of nowhere. I stayed put. My work was here."

"But was it really separatist, in that way?" Laura asked, laying
her hand on Carol's arm. "Any more than any of us are? I mean,
everyone is in their little lives."

She spoke without conviction, attempting to apologize
for Carol, but as Naomi was about to speak Carol launched in
again, taking to task the ideology of personal liberation, the
influence of fundamentalist communism on back-to-the-land
movements, the entrenched misogyny of the radicalism they'd
both subscribed to, and continuing until she'd reached totali-
tarianism and the Soviet Union. Naomi gave up trying to talk;
so did Laura.

As Laura went back to her food she gave Naomi a mutinous
look. Naomi almost winked at her. She remembered that now:
Carol's tendency to skim over particular details in pursuit of her
own thought, to make one thing stand in for another. Besides,
they'd both been, in different ways, apologists for excess, yet
somehow Naomi was now on the other side, unable to see the
extent of their common mistake. The treatment of intellectuals,
of dissidents, the lists of deaths and absences, Carol went on
and on. Naomi knew this was directed at her, but she could not
see how the twentieth century was her fault.

Half listening, she looked around the room. Of course she
made Carol angry. She was untethered to anything Carol could
recognize as a life; her life must be a judgment on Carol herself. She knew it was. But the room was also a declaration of
allegiance, a separation. The pictures, the dusty rows of books

on the dark wood shelves. This chosen group of people, their assumed agreement, their like-mindedness. She was not, in particular, guilty of shutting out the world.

She'd known a man once from New York. He was passing through in secret, and moved on quickly. He called himself Ash; everyone understood he was in trouble, and that this was not his name. Saul, the bell-maker, knew him, Saul vouched for him, and so they hid him for a few weeks. She worked with him in the garden. He was bungling and overconfident. Saul told her casually that Ash didn't like women. At first she thought he meant sexually, then realized it was in general. She, categorically, was something he did not like. This made him aggressively garrulous. Where would he go next? He straightened up, red-eyed and reeking. He would farm, he replied. He had a piece of land in California. If he could get there. He would work the land alone, using only a stick. Why a stick? Because, he answered without irony, he'd studied the history of oppression and decided that, to avoid being allied with the oppressor, he would need to trace it back to the first moment, the foundational moment. She thought of Cain and Abel, spilled blood staining the field. No, he said. The plough. So he would till his land with a stick. There was something in the lone figure, tilling his plot with his stick, that was so forlorn and so courageous that she wished she could tell the story, but she wasn't sure what she wanted to convey. Except that a lost cause might be noble. Of course, she wouldn't be here if she really believed that. She would have stayed.

Laura refilled her glass, stood up to clear the plates. It was time for dessert; Carol at last stopped talking.

Quashed somewhat by the silence that followed her speech, Carol left Naomi alone. Naomi remembered to ask Robert about himself. He said, with a cringing air, that he was a playwright. Pressed, he mentioned some theatres he'd worked with. She'd heard of none of them and could tell from his diffidence that they were well-known. He described his latest play, set in Saskatchewan in the early fifties, which was about to begin rehearsals. Naomi listened with the attention he had a right to expect in return for his display of modesty. He fiddled with the sleeve of his sweater, pulling it down over his hand.

"And he writes poetry," Laura said.

"Oh, please don't tell her that!" he exclaimed, and everyone laughed.

"Why not?" she asked.

He frowned, thinking. "It makes me feel self-conscious," he said. "Seeing myself from the outside."

Naomi left first, thinking of Trout. She tried to leave quietly, but both Carol and Laura followed her into the hall, with Robert trailing disappointed behind them. Laura kissed her cheek; Naomi tensed, feeling herself an object of compassion.

"Come again, come back soon!" Laura said feelingly, making Naomi conscious of how much she must have been a presence, in the way that stories from before lovers meet take on a mythic significance.

She stopped on the corner, thinking of Robert saying he felt self-conscious, of Carol tipsily holding forth on the mistakes of existence, and believed she had spent the evening among people weighing themselves from the outside. Carol thought she was a fanatic, but so was Carol, to be so sure of her own rightness. Or perhaps it was that Carol thought she could comprehend the whole world, and Naomi could only belong to, and know, one place. Unvarying faces attaining slow age. She had left her place. She had lost. She was a stranger. This feeling that her own body was unfamiliar and purposeless lay in wait for her every moment. Her knee protruding from her skirt, her shoulder, her own face in the bathroom mirror. She would stand, waiting until she could figure out how to lift her arm or keep walking. In those times, she thought she should have stayed where she was, in the farmhouse in the midst of her people. Let her child keep the only life she had ever known.

She bent over in the street, winded by the enormity of her bereavement.

She'd left for Trout, which Trout had not asked for. There was no way to undo it now. She could not go back.

Give Trout a year, Naomi thought, and the Other Kingdom would be revoked. *Children are adaptable,* her father said approvingly, as though adaptation were the highest good. Trout would learn to be adaptable. She might even learn to be happy. Perhaps that was what Naomi's father meant by adaptation. To turn resignation into contentment. Maybe that was happiness. Was it?

She would have to begin to believe that her life here was real. She would have to make some plans.

Trout was awake, sitting on the couch next to Harold, who was reading "The Snow Queen." Trout studied the razor wire of snowflakes at the hem of the queen's dress, the blue lips of Kai, his icy hands tying his sled to the gilded sledge. Winters like that would only come in pictures now. Toronto was a few inches of grey snow, barely enough to leave footprints in. She sat down on Trout's other side without taking off her coat, pulled Trout onto her lap. Harold kept reading, his glasses catching the light.

Handful of Dust

THE NETTING THAT LINED MIRANDA'S SKIRT BUNCHED underneath the dark-blue dress, sparked electricity from her thick white tights. A brooch, a circle of plastic pearls, fastened her white collar. The sleeves were too short. She flicked her wrist and the cigarette spattered ash along the bodice. Her eyes were suspicious and crafty behind little glasses.

She was seventeen and I was eighteen, standing together in my bedroom. I had a scholarship and so had a room to myself. It was a small liberal arts college that held on to antiquated distinctions, as mannered as Miranda's aspirations to Victorian girlhood. She came to my room sometimes to smoke cigarettes. Everything in my room smelled like smoke. This was when you could still smoke in a university residence, if you kept the window open.

"Have you accepted Christ?" Miranda asked.

"Yes," I said, and giggled.

"Those who have accepted Christ will be lifted up."

She pulled hard on her cigarette, frowning in satisfaction at the thought of those others, who had not accepted Christ.

She was the first person I had met (that I knew of) who believed in hell. I was studying Classics and English. The after-life in my cosmology was twilight, the river Styx, philosophers and minor heroes wandering dark banks, forgetting. Hell was too literal, too sharp: nothing forgotten, nothing forgiven. I was the first queer she'd met (that she knew of, I added). We regarded each other with a small jolt of excited disgust. The smoke came out of her mouth in yellowish wisps.

We met in the university chapel. She did not belong with or like the catty Anglican divinity students who made up the scant congregation and performed adjacent ceremonies (flower arranging for Easter, drinking sherry after the service, typing newsletters for the elderly minister, who held tightly to the railing when he walked down the chapel steps, his black robes rendering his heavy body sexless) that, like the university itself, had become self-conscious long before they were born. The young men wore vests and ties, the women long cotton or woollen skirts, their hair brusquely pulled back, striving for the haven of middle age, though their cheeks and foreheads were still pocked with acne.

She sat beside me in the pew. Her light-brown hair was furred at the back of her head. Layers of sweater over an old T-shirt, the circle brooch I grew used to, old jeans. We were alone in the pew; everyone else had gone to take communion. Miranda did not take communion. I found out later that her congregation, in the small town in Maine she was from, was much more fire-and-brimstone. I'd never been inside a church before, except for my uncle's wedding. Going to chapel was an aesthetic experiment, like reading Ovid and Plato and Auden. I loved the stained wood and the smell of the hymn books in the same way I loved old movies and vintage clothes and museums. The incense from the gold censer had nothing to do with God. It was a vision of beauty, the murky pendulum of the swinging world.

I stuck out as much as she did in my maroon velvet jacket, black jeans tucked into combat boots, my head shaved so close my scalp shone blue. I painted my nails dark purple and wore a purple neckerchief. I was clownish and half knew it. I smiled and she smiled back, showing the tips of her little teeth.

"Can I have one?" she asked, standing afterwards on the grass in front of the chapel steps.

"How long have you been doing that?" I asked, watching her cup her hand unconvincingly around the cigarette as though it would go out.

"Do you like the *Iliad?*" she replied. I'd taken the paperback out of my bag, hoping to look occupied in case no one spoke to me. I said it wasn't something you liked or disliked. She told me not to be rude. I hated being called rude, rudeness was for children, I was trying to be abrupt. I talked about the lists of names in the *Iliad*, and Simone Weil's essay "The Iliad, or The Poem of Force," which I had read but not understood, and whether Weil was anti-Semitic, and how she'd starved herself in solidarity with the French troops, because at that time her death interested me more than the deaths in Homer, even though they were the same: laudable, useless. Perhaps, when she died, she thought of those lists of names. Weil's faith was something I wanted and wanted others to have. I venerated people who could not navigate the world. I didn't want to fail, but I liked the idea of failures. They seemed to come closest to poetry. Miranda told me her name, I told her mine. She held her hand out. I was not used to shaking hands. Her nails were dirty.

In my bedroom, she dropped her cigarette into the ashtray on the windowsill. Outside, it was dusk. I was still giggling about accepting Christ.

"Don't make fun of me," Miranda said.

"I'm not making fun of you," I said.

She noticed the ash on her bodice and brushed at it, leaving a smear. "Oh, *fuck*," she said, enunciating a word she was trying to get used to.

"Where are you going anyway, in that dress?"

"The Christmas service, aren't you coming?"

"No," I said. I'd stopped going to chapel weeks before, was beginning to make friends, had found a desk in the back row of my *Iliad* course on which someone had painstakingly carved *we read to know we are not alone* and decided I didn't need the incense, I could find that feeling of significance elsewhere.

"You should come," she said stubbornly.

I found a washcloth and took her down the hall to the shared bathroom, fluorescent lit and beige, the cream-coloured grout between the tiles peeled away by compulsive young women late at night. Earlier in the year huge moths whirred in the shower stalls, but they were dead now.

I moistened the washcloth. The drain was threaded with long hairs. I held out the washcloth.

"You do it," she said.

When I was done, there were dark wet patches on the dress. She stood under the dryer, holding the fabric taut. Dried, the patches were still visible, the nap of the velvet pressed the wrong way, turning the blue into grey. She straightened the brooch, looking at herself in the mirror. I stood behind her, watching her purse her lips together, and I was sorry then.

"You should come tonight, get changed," she said, going out.

It was the carol service before the Christmas break. The chapel was full for the first time. Cedar rope ran along the pews, tied by shiny red bows. The choir shuffled in, followed by the choir director, stooped so that his gaze was level with the breasts of the first row of young women. I watched my French professor trying to corral her daughter, who wore a dress that was the same slippery red as the decorative bows. The girl squealed and ran, her face contorted, something congealed on her cheek. The mother smiled at anyone who looked at her, and glanced sometimes at her husband, already settled heavily into his seat. Their marriage was the subject of student gossip. He had been her professor. They had married when she was nineteen and he fifty, twenty years ago. The daughter, adopted from China, was now five. When they married, her parents had threatened a lawsuit and he had taken a year's absence from teaching. Perhaps she had sat silently in his classroom, and decided to eschew the things she was supposed to want (autonomy, liberation), in favour of something thornier. Passion, his gratitude, his guilt. He was married to a woman his own age, they were childless; afterwards, she moved away. I could not imagine anything passionate from the old man, regarding his wife and child with affronted surprise, the child vibrating with purpose, the mother outsmarted. I wonder, now, how often my French professor thought of her former self, sitting in his classroom, willing him to look at her. I think of her, feebly snatching at her daughter, and I feel such pity, though then I thought she was embarrassing, clinging to girlishness, with her shell-pink nails and little voice.

Miranda was sitting beside a middle-aged man with a wan, bony face. Her arm was through his. He had a strained expression that suggested sour breath, a tendency to pronounce his opinions with optimistic finality. When she saw me she put her head down on his shoulder. The choir began to sing.

"This is Roland," she said after the service.

I couldn't quite believe that was the man's name, it was a name someone from the Medieval Reenactment Society would take on. I saw them sometimes in front of the library, laced into badly fitting costumes, waddling happily towards each other with foam-tipped lances, plastic swords.

"Are you visiting?" I asked.

"No," he said, "I live here."

"He's my uncle," Miranda said.

I didn't know what to say to the lie and left for bed.

I stood at the door to the residence, looking out at the quadrangle, thick wet snowflakes catching the orange glow of the central lamp beside the flagpole, melting as soon as they hit the ground. The flag curled around the pole, stirring in the small gusts of wind as if trying to unfurl. It was dingy and ugly. Only the snow was beautiful.

In bed, I thought about Miranda and why she'd lied, and her dress, and her smell of tobacco and something musty, like old cloth.

Then there were exams, and I didn't see her. I'd found an exam study group in a house off-campus. The three girls (Masha, Alex, Val) who lived there were knowing and cruel, saying sarcastic things to each other, already familiar with the Latin and Greek that I would require to finish my degree, though they were all women's studies majors taking the *Iliad* to encounter the patriarchy. There was a piano and rotting flowers in vases, Kathy Acker's *Blood and Guts in High School* in the bathroom beside the filthy toilet. The house was huge, with wide floorboards and pale-green walls and glass doors leading out to the muddy backyard, which had a firepit and a tree house with a rope ladder. I was just interesting enough to be invited, but felt myself to be loud and ungainly, there on sufferance and not sure where their style and self-assertion came from, too naive to understand that it came from money. They were among the truly wealthy, their parents gave to scholarships and capital campaigns, they had grown up with private schools and therapists and trips to Asia and Europe, and though they had eluded their destinies for a while through social outrage and calculated squalor, they had a scornful confidence that still showed their inheritance, gave authority to the way they shouted when they argued, the way they wept when speaking about reproductive rights or the scars and burns that the most beautiful, Masha, had along her arms. Everything they did was queasily dazzling. I wanted to be like them. Like Masha, standing pensively looking out at the tree house, seen through the rain that had replaced the snow, her face opaque, her attention something valuable.

The atmosphere in the house was fraught. I tried to be serious and ironic, someone who understood complex arguments and yet could lay over them an absolute moral certainty, someone who knew where the line of truth was and could know when it moved, castigating those outside. Masha was always on the right side, with her sadness, her smell of jasmine oil and sweat, watching me flounder. She kissed me one night when we were both very drunk, and I hoped she would again (she never did).

I saw her once, a few years ago, sitting on the other side of the playground, where I was with my two sons. We were Facebook friends, I knew she worked for an organization that promoted international food security, was married to a city councillor. I knew she no longer went by Masha, had possibly only adopted the name for a few years. I sometimes scrolled through her life. She sat very straight on the blanket under the trees across the park, talking to her friend. Both of them seemed to gleam with health and purpose, sipping drinks, responding warmly to their children. I didn't approach. I was sleepless, scabby, had just yelled at my youngest so loudly I'd drawn stares from other mothers. Looking at Masha, who was now, again, Natalie, I was tired enough to believe she was immaculate and unshaken. I was taken aback afterwards by how strongly I'd resented her, as if she had no fear, no sense of her life as something beyond her capacity. I tried to explain this feeling to my wife, who smiled faithfully, half listening, waiting until I was finished.

I was sitting in the student lounge, reading without much attention, my mouth bitter from burnt coffee. I had a late exam for the *Iliad* class. The campus was close to empty. An older man sat a few couches away. I could feel him looking at me. The woman who worked at the snacks counter was wiping it down slowly, covering the trays of stale blueberry muffins and waxy apples. I turned my chair to notice if she left so I could follow her. When I looked up, the man was walking over.

"It's Roland," he said, "I'm a friend of Miranda's. We met."

"I thought she said you were her uncle."

There was a pause, as if I'd said something indelicate that he would allow to pass without comment. He sat down across from me.

"Have you seen Miranda?"

"She's gone. Her exams were earlier."

She'd said goodbye when we'd run into each other in the hall, both standing irresolutely, her hand on the door.

"Have a good Christmas," I said.

"You too," she answered, "and may Christ be with you."

She moved forward, and I thought she was going to touch me, and I felt that small jolt again. The door swung wide with the force of her leaving.

"We don't actually know each other that well," I went on, seeing something gather in Roland's face, a request or confession. I wanted neither.

"She's having a difficult transition," he said, the way a teacher might speak about a disruptive child, the way my parents, both high school teachers, spoke to one another about the students they worried over but could not bring themselves to like.

"I don't know her that well," I said again.

"You're her friend," he corrected, "she trusts you."

"What are you?" I asked, still hoping to offend him so he'd go away.

"I am her emotional support," he said gravely.

The woman behind the counter was rinsing out the cloth, getting her bag. I looked at the clock. There was an evening shift, another woman who sold soup cups and rolls. It was always the same two women. They were middle-aged and wore blue eyeshadow and I knew nothing about them. Any minute, I thought, the other woman would arrive.

"I want you to understand that Miranda is experiencing a crisis in her life," he said, and then he looked so desperate that I thought he must love her in a way that made him want to shield her, and that made him assume I loved her too. The woman had left, it was just us in the lounge, under the flickering lights.

"She is experiencing a crisis in her relationship to her family, which I can't give you details about without a serious violation of her privacy, but I think you ought to know that she has had a more difficult time than many people her age, and that she may require specific support. I have become a figure in her life, but she requires more than it's appropriate for me to give her. I thought you might want to know that, so you can be part of her intimate support system."

He stopped speaking. I smiled politely and willed him to go away.

"I know this is not clear to you, but I think she could use more help."

"I'll keep it in mind," I said.

"Thank you," he said.

As Roland buttoned his coat and knotted his scarf, I considered asking him what he actually meant, since everything he'd said seemed like jargon. But that might make him sit back down. He went out as the other woman came in and wiped the counter again.

I spent the week I was still on campus, before I flew home for Christmas, expecting to see Roland somewhere, the man on the opposite side of the road, walking the same way as me when I went to the gas station at midnight to buy cigarettes and candy, a figure just visible in the dark, moving between the street lights. Once, I waited for him to catch me up, like a dare with myself, imagining I was in the middle of a dangerous story, but it wasn't him, and I didn't know what the story was.

Miranda's face came to me in detail, the stains on her teeth, the snarls of uncombed hair. I kept returning to her hair, thinking how it would feel, the smoother strands and the tangles, and the contrast between her little-girl velvet dress and the tangles no longer seemed like a clumsy provocation. She was an animal that could not groom itself, a dog with clumped fur. In my head, we played out a scene which unfolded straightforwardly, involving banal scenarios that I'd never experienced: rain, sudden tears, an abrupt move towards each other, none of the awkwardness that the real thing, happening between us as we were, would have had.

I didn't think about her at night, only in the daytime when I was supposed to be studying, looking away from my desk and out the window.

I want to say now that I am a fairly happy person. My life has turned out well. There has been work and marriage and children. I follow the news in various forms, I negotiate, as we all do, a fractious tension between the virtual and the physical world, I cook, I sometimes travel with my family. We live in a pleasant house on a pleasant street in a large city, and I know some of my neighbours well enough to speak to them and to worry about them and discuss them in detail with my wife and our friends. But I find myself returning to Miranda because I am now old enough to experience a nebulous, sly regret. I am very fortunate (I say this often), and part of my good fortune is fullness. I don't have much experience of loneliness, after all, only the occasional bleakness of feeling myself alone in a way that no person can help, and I'm not an idiot, I know that is common to everyone, yet at those times I think of Miranda, and imagine her life as another kind of loneliness, more profound, more persistent. That's patronizing, I know, assuming that her life continued on as lonely as it seemed to me then. But when I think of her, I envy her imagined solitude, the focus and clarity of her days, as though she got the future I envisioned for myself when I knew her, in which I strode, mythological, across wet grass, my life only in my head. It's an adolescent fantasy, born out of books, it's meant to be replaced by other things: obligations, my aging parents, my two sons, the familiar body of my wife, the tasks that accrue living in a house.

I think this is connected to God, something I wonder about more, these days. Though I suspect I think of God acquisitively, as something I want and feel I deserve, not so different from the promise offered by new shoes or a new book to read or a new show to watch. A wistful hope, which exists only briefly, for absolute solace.

When I think of Miranda, I envy her faith, which she probably had not even kept; so few people do. I envy it as something that would give meaning to loneliness, instead of my experience of a sudden lurch, the gap in a nightmare, falling, falling.

I teach literature part-time at a community college. I like the classes and the students, though I dislike the institution, which seems grasping and self-congratulatory. But the subject matter throws this feeling of falling into terrible relief. I stood recently in front of my class, quoting *I will show you fear in a handful of dust* and paused imperceptibly, in terror at what that meant: the possibility that the world and our life in it is only material, only dust.

The *Iliad* exam was over. Masha, Alex, and Val were stoned in their kitchen, passing around a bottle of Glenlivet. I don't think any of them had eaten anything. I leaned against the counter, half-welcome, and told them about Roland. In my telling, Miranda (whom I'd never mentioned before) was a fragile enigma, potentially threatened by whatever trouble Roland hinted at, or by Roland himself, or both.

"So, what are you going to do?" Masha asked, passing me the bottle.

"I don't know," I said.

"You need to confront her," Masha said. Murmurs around the table.

"I don't think that's what he meant," I said.

"It doesn't matter, he disclosed something, he almost disclosed something."

In the fug of smoke (the only light in the kitchen was a cluster of stubby candles stuck to a placemat in the centre of the table), I nodded.

Walking home, my head cleared, but I suspected I had made a promise, and pressed my hand over the knot in my stomach.

The knot continued all through Christmas break when I thought of Miranda, and was still there as the plane descended. The airport was small, and for most of the descent all I could see below were thick, dark trees. What would I say? What was supposed to happen?

She opened the door before I knocked.

"Are you on your way out?" I asked.

"I knew someone was there," she said.

"Can I come in?"

She stood aside.

I'd never been inside her room. Miranda didn't like her roommate. Alison was studying journalism and had taken time off to travel after high school, her extra two years giving her an air of adult seriousness. She was on the student union and I'd seen her speak once at a protest, scrubbed square face, blond spirals escaping her ponytail. I could picture her backpacking somewhere, sensible in blue fleece, navigating train stations, unfamiliar cities and mountains, churches and temples, interested, unsentimental.

There was a line of black tape across the floor.

"I put that there," Miranda said, "so we didn't have to argue anymore."

"About what?"

"The walls. She said I was putting stuff up on her side, so I measured."

I imagined Miranda on her knees, spitefully measuring. I stood experimentally on the line, looking at the room. On one side Alison's textbooks lined a pine board shelf, beside a bed with a jumble of blankets. Her walls were almost bare. A family photograph, a mock construction sign that read DANGER WOMEN WORKING.

Miranda sat down on her bed, gestured at her desk chair. "Sit if you like," she said ungraciously.

Her side of the room was profuse and precious. Dried petals lined the top of her dresser, interspersed with prisms that looked as if they'd been unhooked from an old chandelier, and her mirror had a piece of white cloth slung above it, the glass half-covered. I went and sat on the edge of the bed, ignoring the chair. She drew her knees up to her chin and pressed herself into the corner, her feet on her pillow.

The bed was made up with a quilt in pink-and-blue squares, each square with a tuft of white acrylic wool sewn into the centre. The wall beside the bed was crowded with overlapped pictures, reaching as far as the edge of the mirror and almost to the ceiling. I'd expected Bible verses, but it was mostly kitschy Pre-Raphaelite paintings: Ophelia drowning, the Lady of Shallot, Isabella and the Pot of Basil, each of them a man's evocation of the lovely despair of a woman.

"Your parents?" I asked, touching the edge of a portrait of a man and woman who could not be anyone else, standing on either side of Miranda with their hands pressing her shoulders.

"What did Roland tell you?" she asked.

"What?"

"Roland. He talked to you."

"He told you?"

"Of course he *told* me."

"He asked if I could help you."

"What did he say?"

I tried to remember his words. "He said you were having a crisis in your family life. He said you were undergoing a crisis, a personal crisis. He said he was your emotional support, but that you needed more."

"Meaning you?"

"I guess," I said miserably.

She tilted her head to one side almost archly, waiting for me to say more.

"What else did he tell you?" she asked at last.

"What else?"

"Did he say how I met him?"

"How did you meet him?"

"He's a sexual surrogate. Do you know what that is?"

I had an idea of myself as a radical, and I wasn't a virgin, but Roland was so at odds with any way I was willing to think about sex, with his folds of middle-aged skin and his long fingers and complacent monotone. I must have looked aghast, though I tried to hide it, wanting to seem sophisticated, as she now did.

"Are you—are you one of Roland's clients?"

"No, of course not. The age difference is too big, he wouldn't take me as a client. Anyway, I can't have sex and I don't want to. He runs a group I'm part of. We meet once a month. It's a talking group. We got to be friends. I don't have a lot of friends. I guess he thought I needed more, and he remembered you. So. Do you think I need your help?"

"I don't know."

"Did he tell you anything about my parents?"

I shook my head, humiliated.

"Good. He doesn't know anything about my parents. He imagines things."

She knew I did as well.

She leaned over and touched my knee. "I have a bunch of work to do," she said, but didn't withdraw her hand. She traced her fingers to a point just above my knee, so lightly it would have been easy to interpret it as the prelude to taking her hand away. Then she squeezed my thigh, a mean pinching motion, and got up.

"I don't need your help with anything," she said.

I stood. Trying to be casual, I tiptoed along the black line, stopped so I was facing her.

She kissed me. It was as sudden as I'd imagined and nothing like I'd imagined: inept, disgusted. She drew back and wiped her mouth.

"Shit," I said softly.

She shook her head, as if I hadn't understood.

There was another picture that I hadn't noticed before, which I saw now behind her left shoulder, since I couldn't manage to look her in the face. It was an Impressionist street scene. Evening, lamps flaring in the grey rain. A boulevard with horse-drawn carriages, couples walking, and off to one side, a figure in black walking alone, his back to the viewer. He wasn't even the focus of the picture, but I remembered him for years, though I never saw the picture again. He reminded me of Miranda herself, someone whose face I could never see. When I think of this figure, I feel shame. Not exactly sexual shame (so much is made of sexual shame, but I often think that's the least of our worries), but something else, something to do with the shame of presuming to help someone without knowing anything about them, without humility, as though other people were there only to bolster my good opinion of myself.

"I have a bunch of work to do," she said, and I left.

I didn't tell Masha or the others anything. I don't know if they were disappointed that I didn't bring up Miranda again or that there was no sequel involving a straightforward victim whom they could help me to save. They probably lost interest; they lost interest in me soon afterwards.

I avoided Miranda for a week, which was easy: we weren't in any classes together and lived in different wings of the residence hall. Then I decided to find her, not sure yet what I would do. Apologize. Kiss her back. Ask her what it was I didn't understand.

Alison was pulling up the tape from the floor of their room.

"Is Miranda here?"

"Miranda went home," she said, looking over her shoulder, crouched down and scraping with her thumbnail at the tape's gummy track. "She had some kind of family problem, I think."

"Is she coming back?"

"If she does I'm asking to be moved. She drove me crazy. Praying all the time."

She stood up, rolled the tape into a ball, and threw it at the wastebasket. It missed and stuck to the wall.

"Do you want her email? She left her email in case she left anything behind. She did leave stuff, actually, but I'm getting rid of it. It was just some junk."

"No, thanks."

I couldn't think of anyone to ask why she'd gone. I couldn't think of anyone who was her friend. Sometimes I eyed the Anglicans picking their way through the thawing mud on the chapel steps, but they wouldn't have known either. I didn't know how to approach them. I had not disliked them as much as Miranda had, I'd just grown tired of my posturing, but looking at them I felt hatred, as though they were the reason she'd left, the reason she was spiky and unskillful and desolate.

Alison put a box of Miranda's stuff outside beside the garbage bins. I noticed it the next day. It had rained in the night, and the pictures at the top were stuck together, sodden and curling. Pushing them aside, I found a pamphlet underneath: *Where Will You Be on the Day of Judgment?* Brutally coloured, bisected by a faded line of fire. Above, the saved strolled through paradise under spreading trees, the sun yellow forever, and below, other people in a dark pit drowned in some kind of liquid. The walls of hell were brownish pink, ribbed, the damned the undigested contents of a stomach. I sat on the curb and made myself read it. It was blunt, ungrammatical.

It was what she believed. I didn't know if she thought I was damned, or if she was.

I was about to toss the pamphlet back, but instead folded it into my jacket pocket. I put it on my desk, then in a drawer. I took it out again and wrote *Miranda* in the top-left corner, so that no one could think it belonged to me. When I was clearing out the desk at the end of the year, I found the pamphlet and this time I threw it away, tearing it first into small pieces.

I know Alison slightly. She works for a national newspaper; I read and enjoy her columns. She is thorough and knowledgeable about Toronto, where we are both from and to which we returned. My wife works for a charitable foundation that gives money to civic-minded projects, and the foundation was once involved in a minor expense scandal. Alison interviewed her and was respectful and fair. The foundation weathered the scandal and no one was fired except for a man they wanted to fire anyway.

We ran into each other at a book launch for a mutual friend, which we had both come to alone. She leaned against the bar while we chatted, mostly about children, though she didn't have any and I was afraid I was boring her, but children were the subject with which I felt helplessly identified.

Her hair was short now, her red cardigan and pencil skirt an obvious progression from her primary fleeces and jeans, and she had the same unostentatious friendliness tinged with impatience. She worked in, bashfully pleased to tell me, that her partner was a woman (I could just remember her boyfriend, standing beside her at protests, his placard slung over his shoulder), and this seemed to me another part of her sensible trajectory, to which a wife would be better suited than a husband. A practicality and tidiness that would fit with what she wanted (it wasn't true in my case: my wife and I used to have extravagant fights, terrible silences), though it wasn't as if I had ever known her well, not enough to be so condescending, but just then I was depleted and unkind and didn't like myself very much.

"Remember Miranda?" I said.

She nodded, frowning. "It's funny. She emailed me about a year ago. She found my work email online. She wrote *Remember me* in the subject line, so I didn't open it, I thought it was a virus. But then she wrote again."

"So what convinced you to open it?"

"The subject line was different. *It's Miranda (black line of tape in the middle of the room).* So I opened it."

"What did it say?"

"Oh, she just wanted to apologize for being a jerk," she said, stirring the ice in her glass.

There was more; I waited.

"She wanted to explain. Why she left. I don't know why she thought I was still thinking about it."

"Did you ever think about it?"

"No, I didn't," Alison said, surprised by my tone. Then she went on.

When I thought about it later, I decided from the way Alison said it that Miranda must have used the word *rape*, not *sexual assault*, at once technical and vague, so broadly applicable as to risk a loss of meaning. Miranda would have been stringent, primal, Biblical, brief. When her mother refused to believe her, she went to her aunt's and never spoke to her parents again. She did not complete university, and now worked in a Christian bookstore in a small town across the country from the town in Maine she'd come from. Her mother was dead; it was because of her cancer diagnosis that Miranda had gone home. Her father might still be living. She had decided it was better not to know.

"But why did she want to tell you?" I asked.

Alison shook her head, her sleek cap of wiry gold hair absorbing the glow from the Edison bulbs strung over the bar. She looked dejected, wishing she'd never brought it up.

"I don't know. She said it was on her mind. But she seemed so *sorry*. I don't know why she was so sorry. I wrote back. I told her I was shocked to hear about what she'd gone through, that I wished her well. It was a short message. I was busy. I didn't know what to say. She wrote again. This long, long message about the will of God."

"Did you answer?" I knew I was accusing her and it wasn't fair.

"I didn't. I should, but I didn't."

There was a pause in which we both wished for words.

"Thank you for telling me," I said at last, formally.

The reading began and we moved away from each other to find seats.

I left before she did, going down the steps of the Gladstone Hotel. The restaurants along Queen Street were full, artfully lit. Thinking of Miranda, I almost believed I would see her coming towards me. Tangled hair, tiny glasses, monk-like hunch to her walk, emerging from the sooty darkness under the bridge as I crossed Dufferin Street. There were several candidates, figures approaching, but each one was, of course, someone else.

At home, I located her easily on the staff page of the bookstore where she worked, Living Waters Books and Coffee. The image on the main page was neutral, a pleasant, light-filled space with shelves to the ceiling, an ornate brass ladder on wheels, two armchairs turned towards each other. A granite counter with gleaming espresso machine, rows of squat white cups and saucers, trays of biscotti along the back wall. A stencilled cross in black above the sink.

She was heavier, drooping, the little glasses replaced by thicker ones with green plastic frames. Her hair was smooth, loose over her shoulders. She was not quite smiling, but one corner of her mouth turned up. She'd recently been staff person of the month. She liked J.R.R. Tolkien, murder mysteries, good coffee, and the music of Sufjan Stevens. The Bible presumably went without saying.

I stared at her picture, hoping no one yet knew I was home. I could hear the sounds of bedtime upstairs, my wife reading to our eldest son in his orange-and-yellow-painted room, the lamp with the acrobats on the shade switched on over their heads, beside the mobile with its little felt birds and wooden flowers that still hangs above him as he sleeps.

"Is that you?"

"I'm coming!" I called, shutting my laptop, turning out the light.

The next day, I stopped at the church across the street from my children's school. It was large, Catholic, built in the nineteenth century. I went up the steps, intending to sit for a moment in one of the pews. I was early for pickup and the day was cold.

I pushed open the heavy door, moving carefully in the silence. The air smelled of incense. There were two homeless men asleep, stretched full out on the pews across the aisle, their bags piled around them. A few rows ahead of me, a young man sat, his head lowered, but I couldn't tell if he was praying or dozing.

I didn't want to pray and didn't know how, so I sat with my hands resting on the curved back of the pew in front and looked up at the geometric holy shapes painted in turquoise and gilt far above me.

A woman came in. She was older than me, but not yet old. She walked quickly, crossing herself as she walked. When she reached the steps leading up to the altar she knelt and touched her forehead to the stone, stood, and knelt again, touching her forehead to the stone, standing, kneeling, bowing her head. Penance, I supposed, though I didn't know anything about it. Down went her forehead, pressing the stone over and over, matter-of-fact, as if this was an ordinary action, available to anyone, to me.

A Beautiful Bare Room

THE SCREEN, FRAMED LIKE A WINDOW, SHOWED SEPIA wheat and a grey sky. The wheat was beaded with rain. The screen was thoughtfully curated. Sometimes what she saw was real, the actual field above their heads, and sometimes not: a painting, a picture of a landscape. She hadn't asked if the switch was automated or if a person, somewhere above, was conscripted to observe what was going on outside and decide when the sight (a child with an empty face, dark rain) was too much to bear.

It seemed bearable today. Ordinary rain. Wheat fields.

Liza had not thought of herself as a person who would end up in the bunker. She hadn't known places like the bunker existed, though she'd imagined, when she thought of it, that the super-rich had made provisions for the shit hitting the fan. But she was so far away from making escape plans, living with Erin in their tiny rooms, working their small jobs. There was no point thinking about it. Erin was good at not thinking about it. *A real pea souper,* Erin would say in a terrible approximation of a British accent (she'd liked old Sherlock Holmes movies, the murky, villainous streets), waving her hand at the window on days when the smog was so thick they couldn't see the building opposite. Erin, with her horsey laugh and scabs on her arms from scratching and her lapsed fundamentalism, which she retained as an almost perverse cheerfulness, an insistence that everything would be fine, even if Jesus wasn't coming. Standing in the doorway making faces at Liza. Eating cereal together moistened with water when milk was no longer available, both of them hunched over the bowls in their underwear at the card table in the kitchen. The water ran yellow out of the tap. And even that, apparently, could not keep Erin from hopefulness. My one and only, Liza thought, because Erin used to call her that when she texted to say she'd be late from the bar. *My one and only*. Sometimes *my best and only*. Erin knew that the way to get through was to make everything a joke. She used to put her hand on the back of Liza's neck, saying *just checking, just checking*, pretending she was feeling for the raised rash that was the first symptom, when the government finally admitted that yes, this was happening, it was not a rumour, these were the signs. Erin's fingers spread on her neck. Erin was probably dead now, in the ruins of Palo Alto. Unless it wasn't ruined. Unless Liza should have stayed. She had lost track of how long she had been in the bunker. Two months? Four? Six? Lulled by the bland affluence around her, the steady stream of comforts. And they were so deep underground.

She'd arrived with Neal in a car after more than five hours on the road. She was bad at gauging direction, and some of the lights on the highway had burned out. The entrance to the compound was a hole in a rise in the field that Neal had turned the car into, the wheat clinging to the windows, stalks silver in the moonlight. He'd opened the door and pulled her out. The plywood that covered the hole scraped metal as he kicked it away. Under the plywood, a sheet of corrugated iron. Anyone who came upon it would think it was an old well or buried machinery.

"Get that out of the way," he told her. He walked back to the car as she struggled; it was heavier than it looked. A splattering sound behind her. She turned and saw Neal pouring gas on the front seat of the car.

"What are you doing?"

"It's not enough to make it explode. This isn't a movie. I just want it to burn."

"Why?"

"So it looks like a burnt-out car in a field."

She'd finally managed to move the metal. Underneath, a steel door. The car was burning behind her, warming her back. She had no idea where she was. The door opened.

"Liza! Come on."

He walked through. She paused, looking around her. The flames were higher now.

She walked through.

It was still raining on the sepia field. She could hear Neal arguing with his wife, Sally. His face would be red, she knew, but only around the nose and cheeks. She'd pointed that out to him once, how easily his face flushed, and he was so unexpectedly hurt she thought he must love her. Now, not sure why she was here at all, she thought it was more trivial. Her watching him made him feel foolish, and he was not used to that.

She should never have met him. She was a server in a café that she would have thought beneath his notice, not shabby enough to be authentic, not designed enough to offer what he would think of as an experience. But he'd come in, bouncing in his sneakers, in the middle of his run. He ran alone every day, almost like an ordinary person. This was before the silvery rashes started appearing, with everything that followed. Though there were markers that set him apart: the expensive athletic gear, the gas mask, that the exposed parts of his skin showed no scabs, no discolorations. He went running in that neighbourhood to prove something: his egalitarianism, his invulnerability. That he was so fortunate he could afford to be careless.

Once inside the café, he didn't know what to do. He leaned against the counter and then moved back from it, asked her questions as the espresso machine hissed, and she didn't answer, she hadn't heard him. She brought him his coffee, knocked it as she set it down so it slopped into the saucer, then offered him another one.

Later, when they were in the bunker, she told him she'd spilled the coffee on purpose, so he would keep talking to her. She wanted him to feel that she was someone he was meant to have and would keep. After they'd arrived that night, he'd shown her to her room and shown no further interest in her, smiling at her as he passed or making conversation at dinner as if she were an acquaintance who he was determined would not take up too much of his time. Even if she'd wanted to, she didn't know how to get out; if she had to stay here, love or some version of it was her best chance at survival.

But really she had no idea why he'd wanted her in the first place, and she hadn't jostled the cup on purpose. She'd barely noticed him at all.

Perhaps she was a contrast to Sally, to the women in the bunker. If Erin had been in the bunker with her they would have laughed at them, called them trophy wives, which Liza knew they weren't. Most of these women had PhDs, were the CEOs of their own tech companies, had founded business empires based on the fusion of medical expertise and esoteric knowledge. They were not unfriendly, but their friendliness was focused and strategic, tied to goals, to optimal outcomes and best practices. They did not indulge in irony. Irony felt like a jettisoned extravagance here, useless as joy. She remembered lying on her bed with Erin, eating chips, chip crumbs falling into the creases of her neck, and that was joy. She wished she'd known it at the time. These women made her feel hazy and incompetent, though competence was not required of her. There was nothing for her to do.

Liza was twenty-two. She slouched and crossed her arms, her black hair hanging low over one eye, shaved halfway up her scalp on the other side. She would be plump when she was older (Neal calculated everything he ate, taut as a snake) and did not care. Her hair was growing out now, what had been shaved close becoming a pelt, and it was one of the only ways she'd marked how the time passed underground. Her body felt lax and suspect compared with the vigorous people around her. Their health seemed immaculately designed, like the sound of running water that was piped through the corridors, more evidence of their ruthless pursuit of the best, but they would probably have admitted that, if pressed; they were not without self-awareness. They knew they were ruthless. She did not want to press. She was with the victors. She should consider herself lucky. Sometimes she did.

In the field onscreen, a bedraggled girl came into view, moving slowly, her face blurred with the dreaminess that they had all learned to recognize and avoid, out there in the world. The screen flickered, and the child was replaced with another child, blond and female and dressed in white, clutching a bunch of daisies. Liza settled more deeply into the armchair, sentimentally distracted by the digital child and the flowers. She knew it wasn't the real outside, but everything inside the bunker also seemed unreal: the prompt appearance of food and drink, her enormous bed with the white sheets. The two armchairs drawn up to either side of the screen/window, the deep-blue-and-red rug under her feet, the polished dark oval of the coffee table with a few glossy books of architectural photography and views of national parks fanned out over it, all seemed calculated to make her feel she was living in a dream. A designed dream, general as a high-end real estate magazine. This warren of rooms at her disposal, this munificence of good design, brilliant planning, unthinkable money. She couldn't quite make herself wish she'd stayed outside, but she felt her sense of herself slipping away along with her sense of time, the luxury around her draining her out slowly. Her response to the beautiful child and the solace she took in the deep rug was automatic, as if she was performing a function involuntarily, not understanding why.

She didn't know if staying in Palo Alto would have enabled her to retain some sense of herself as private and personal. Probably not. But her salvation tasted flat in her mouth. She touched the screen. It was cool as winter glass under her hand.

Liza enjoyed working in the café. She had been good at it. She chatted with the lonely and knew when to retreat. There were many regulars, approximately youthful men mulling over Big Data on their laptop screens. She flirted and retained once-mentioned details, knew that even social engineers had lives in which they were as puzzled and yearning as anyone else. They had secret selves, just as she did. She liked to picture herself in the 1970s, as if she was a character in a movie. Standing behind a bead curtain. Barefoot in long grass. A little bit dirty, filching money from a succession of undifferentiated lovers. Dancing alone to earnest ethereal music. She wasn't sure where this vision of herself came from, unless it was from her mother's stories of growing up in a ramshackle commune in Maine. But the fantasy fortified her. She retreated into it in the months before she met Neal, as her phone whirred new government alerts that made it clear how thoroughly and specifically the movement of each person was now being tracked, though the nature of the infection was not yet clear.

In her head, she was alone behind a bead curtain. She was someone who could be alone.

She'd known, almost from the beginning, about Neal's wife. She looked through his wallet after the second time they had sex, brazenly picked out his identity card and held it up beside his cheek, squinting as if to spot a resemblance between his eye and the image of his iris. Gold dot in the corner, black-bordered: he had a greater freedom of movement than she did, just below military-grade. She was only a blue dot. She twisted away from him, staring at the card, memorizing his full name. He was already twitchy, eager to get up. After he left, they looked at him on Erin's phone. There he was, over and over, standing beside Sally. Scalded under his thinning hair, covering his affront at having to appear at these dinners in aid of the Democratic Party, gay rights in what used to be called Eastern Europe, balls that raised funds for ocean regeneration. She could picture him practising an acceptable smile in front of the mirror. Sally's smile was practised enough to be genuine.

Erin said Sally was very beautiful; Liza thought she was too symmetrical, that there was something parched about her. Liza lay back, settled her head onto Erin's shoulder, admired her own smell, her cavalier armpit stubble and frayed underwear. They were superior to the influential people in the pictures, even in their three boxy rooms in one of the most polluted parts of the city, far from the private gardens and clearer air. Liza woke with a pain in her chest every morning, gagged up mucus into the toilet. But right then, her head under Erin's chin, making fun of a woman they would never meet, Liza was convinced they were both indestructible. Erin knew everything would be fine.

Neal told her she would see Dr Azarian every two weeks. She went when the bracelet she wore lit up green, not able to count the days. Seeing Dr Azarian was routine, Neal told her. Establishing a routine was important, it would help her to settle in. She didn't know what would happen once they'd decided she'd settled in. More of the same, forever.

"If anything's wrong, we can catch it early," Dr Azarian said now, turning away while she settled herself into the stirrups.

"But what could you do about it?"

"Oh, anything."

"Anything?" she said, trying to match his tone.

"There's a full surgery down here. And a full pharmacy. We could live here for a hundred years. Or put ourselves under and out if we wanted to."

"Did you used to talk to your patients like that?"

"Nope. I've developed a new bedside manner."

She propped herself up on her elbows. He was lanky, unvarnished. She thought, with some longing, that he didn't quite fit.

"So, what brought you here?" she asked.

"Isn't it obvious?"

"Survival?"

"It's not what I expected."

"What did you expect?"

"They told me my family could come too." He watched her face change. "Sweetheart, I'm totally fucking with you. I don't have a family."

"I'm sorry."

"Why?" he asked, drawing out the speculum. "I didn't want a family."

"Oh."

"I had a boyfriend," he conceded, "but he didn't want to come with me."

"But didn't he *know*? What could happen to him?"

"Yes. Smart guy. But he said he'd rather take his chances on infection than end up with these people and bored out of his mind."

"So what isn't what you expected?"

"That he'd be right."

They eyed each other.

"Do you ever think about leaving?" she asked, pulling on her jeans, crumpling the paper cover in her hand.

"You think we can just *leave?*" he asked, looking down to type something on her chart.

Not sure what to do with herself (so many hours left before sleeping, and she was never much of a reader, even with the enormous library), she went to the armchair and watched the window. It was a stand of trees today, beside a lake in autumn. Nothing happened among the trees except sometimes a red or yellow leaf drifted through the air and rippled out the surface of the lake. She counted the seconds it took for the ripples to reach the shore. There was a thin mist over the lake.

She shifted in the chair. She felt bloated, cramped, like she was about to get her period. At home, she and Erin would have sat around all day if they weren't working, drinking tea and eating candy until they were both sick. She felt sick. At least she wasn't pregnant, she thought. The first few nights, she'd waited in bed, assuming he would come in, but he never did.

She didn't even want him to, very much. But she'd assumed he would. Wasn't that the reason she was there? It must be some other reason. Soon, she would ask him what it was, if she could muster the energy to figure out the right tone. She could not risk a fight or even an argument. Liza would be pliant and quiet. Her skin was so soft now, she passed time by rubbing creams into her face and legs and shoulders that she found in her bathroom in drawers that slid open silently. Outside, she had always been itchy, though she was better than Erin about not scratching.

She watched the leaves fall. Yellow, brown, gold, red. The mist was clearing now. The sun was higher. It would burn the mist away.

Cara came in, talking on her headset. Cara was Sally's business partner, running the technical side of what Liza had heard Neal refer to as Integrated Wellness. Cara gave Liza a watery smile. She would start crying in a minute, Liza knew from experience, tears slipping down her face that she wouldn't wipe away. She would behave as if they didn't belong to her.

Cara was talking to her wife, Angeline, who now existed only as a virtual consciousness. Cara, who had perfected the process, preferred to call it a transferred consciousness. Angeline had become infected, could not come to the bunker. Cara had considered remaining outside with her, putting herself in the way of infection, so at least they could be together. The transfer was still experimental. But Angeline had persuaded her to take the risk. Afterwards, Angeline jumped off the roof of their house. Cara had told all this to Liza almost as soon as she met her, and Liza had not known why. Cara clasped Liza's hand

in both of her own, telling her the story, and wept so gently
that Liza wished she could weep as well, to cement whatever
understanding seemed to now exist between them, which it
might be useful to cultivate.

Cara spent most of her time on the headset or in front of
a large screen that spanned one wall of her room, on which the
image of Angeline appeared, burnished in a tranquil purgatory:
white walls and wood floor, a slate fountain half-visible through
a doorway to a courtyard. Cara had brought Liza to her room
to introduce Angeline.

"Here she is. Look, Angie. Isn't she pretty?"

Angeline waved.

"Nice to meet you," Liza said.

"Oh, I'm not really me anymore," Angeline said, still waving.

"You will be," Cara said, tearing up.

Angeline nodded complaisantly. She shimmered at her
edges, dark hair prismatic in the sunlight from the window to
her left. She looked a little like Liza herself, if Liza had been
taller, thinner, better groomed. Liza wondered if this was an
effect of existing only onscreen, or if (this seemed likely) the
real Angeline had been so poised, so elegant. She was wearing
a long blue dress. She was as pleasing as the landscapes Liza
watched from her favourite armchair.

"I'll figure it out," Cara said.

"I know you will. Of course you will."

"How was Bobby?" Cara asked, settling into the chair across
from Liza.

"Who's Bobby? Did I meet him yet?"

"Dr Azarian."

"He didn't tell me his first name."

"It's Bobby."

"Nobody tells me anything," Liza said, not caring if she sounded sullen.

"Hold on a minute, love," Cara said into the headset.

Angeline murmured something inaudible. The purring tone felt artificial to Liza. Cara was fooling herself, thinking the voice or the vision onscreen was real. Liza was familiar with Angeline now. Cara often brought Liza in to sit in front of the screen, saying Angeline got bored and wanted new faces. Liza tried to amuse. Maybe she was there to be amusing to languid virtual people, if the distinction between virtual and actual was meaningful anymore. Angeline's smile was real. It was cunning. Liza doubted that digital consciousness was capable of secrets. Unanticipated capacities, perhaps, but not the intimate human tendency to conceal schemes. A machine didn't need to do that. A machine was self-sufficient.

"This must be difficult for you," Cara said, patting the arm of the chair with one silky hand.

"Why?"

"You know. Younger, odd one out, Sally, that's a complicated situation and she's a complicated person, we all know each other, you pick."

"What's Angeline saying?" Liza asked.

Cara switched the volume off. "Bobby's a great guy. I've known him for twenty years."

"Oh."

"We dated in college. We're both pretty far along the Kinsey scale, so it was kind of a non-starter, but we stayed close. We have similar research interests."

"But he's a doctor."

"Yes, he is."

"How long have you known Sally?" Liza asked.

"She's my sister. Didn't Neal tell you?"

"No."

Cara stood up, the conversation over. She switched the headset back on. The voice returned; Angeline had never stopped talking. The same soothing rhythm, like the low rush of water from the slate fountain. Cara touched Liza's face as she left, lingering over her cheek, as if appreciating how soft Liza's skin was now, from all the time she spent massaging those pastel creams in before the mirror. It was nice to have someone notice. It was nice to be touched.

The further Liza was from the outside, the more she tried to persuade herself that coming to the bunker had been inevitable. A story that could only have reached one conclusion: these rooms below what had been farmland. Thinking of this story as an impeccably finished thing, like the design of the rooms, helped her to push away the question of whether she'd been a coward, whether she might have stayed where she was and waited for Erin. Been loyal, been brave. If she considered it too much, she thought, her regret would be so huge that she would never move again.

When the predicted surge in infections came, she and Erin barricaded the door and sat looking out the window at the street. They saw people walking, running. They saw slower walkers: the infected. The apartment was on the seventh floor. High enough to be safe if they kept the door shut, too high to spot the raised silver rash on the back of the neck.

"I wonder what it's like?" Liza asked, watching a young woman waft along the sidewalk, holding her skirt up in one hand like a little girl.

"It looks peaceful."

"What would you do if you felt the rash?"

"I'd jump out the window," Erin said. "I'd ask you to drown me in the bathtub."

"That's a waste of water."

"Okay. But you could definitely push me off the balcony."

"You wouldn't even see what happens afterwards?"

"No. I'd rather die."

"Why?"

Liza expected something flippant, that Erin would show her she was only joking, again, but Erin didn't even smile, watching the walkers below.

"Too much like church. Look at them, look at their faces. They all look so sure. I'd rather just be dead."

Liza hoped Erin was dead, after Erin had been missing for five days. Erin didn't exaggerate. She'd rather be dead than transformed into that beatific strangeness. Outside, the infected moved as elegantly as dancers, apparently enjoying the sunshine, all their doubts quieted. Liza thought she could make out the rash now, in strong light, but maybe she was imagining it.

"Liza! Let me in!"

She sat in the dark on the sixth night. It seemed safer with the lights off.

"It's me!"

There was no food left. She'd filled the bathtub with yellow water. She dipped a measuring cup in at intervals, just enough to keep herself going. Her lips were cracking. The water tasted of sulphur.

"Open the door!"

She knew the voice, but she wanted it to go away. It wasn't the voice she wanted. She hugged her knees to her chest in the dark.

"Liza! Come on!"

The high-rises across the street showed lights in some of the windows, flashlights or candles. People like her, alone in locked rooms. The lights flared, receded. Tiny pricks of flame. She hoped they had candles somewhere. Erin would have known where, which kitchen drawer. She didn't know how much longer the electricity would stay on. She didn't want to flick the switch and find darkness was no longer a choice.

As a child, she'd had a game of burning paper in the firepit in her backyard, staring at the embers teeming on its underside as she turned it over, like the movement of ants when she lifted a log in the woods. Not woods, she'd never been in the woods, but the small cluster of trees behind her little yellow house.

The knocking became pounding, then kicking.

She opened the door, her hand on the back of her neck, as if already feeling the raised pattern.

Erin had gone to look for food. They'd split the last of the cereal. Erin got up, pulled out a box from under her bed, lifted out a Swiss Army knife and a small crowbar. Placed them by the door. She did not say that everything would be fine, but Liza thought she still saw the same zany optimism.

"Don't go," Liza said.

"One of us has to," Erin answered, not as if she expected Liza to offer. Liza didn't.

"Don't go," she said again.

Erin kissed her cheek. "I love you," she said.

"I love you too."

A silence.

"Remember me really well," Erin said. She picked up the crowbar and pocketed the knife and was gone.

"Don't open the door to anyone that isn't me!" she called from the hall, and Liza heard the door to the stairs sigh shut. She slid the deadbolt into place.

Neal fell against her and she helped him to stand. Red eyes, sour breath, stubble.

"What took you so fucking long?"

He went on without waiting for an answer. She had to trust him. He'd planned this for years. A strategically chosen group of people. Every eventuality projected. Greenhouses. Medicines. She had ten minutes to pack.

"What about Sally?"

"It was Sally's idea."

"She doesn't know me."

"She knows about you, though," he said.

She left the door unlocked in case Erin forgot her key. Erin always forgot her key.

Sometimes in the bunker she had dreams, real dreams, where Erin came back. Unscathed and with a full bag. Chips, those little cupcakes with rainbow sprinkles and synthetic icing that she'd loved. Some lake water, silted with grey sand, algae. They could strain it, boil it. She'd ease the backpack off her shoulders, look for Liza. On the balcony, in the bathroom, in the bed, under the bed. She'd whisper, preserving the quiet. Expecting Liza to leap out at her, try to surprise her in some stupid way that only Erin would want.

In the dream, Erin kept looking for her, turning round and round like a dog, her smile slipping as she circled.

Liza must have fallen asleep on the examining table. Sleep overtook her almost anywhere now. In the chair in front of the screen, in the sauna, even at dinner, her eyes closing.

She sat up.

"Lie down, kiddo, I'm not finished."

She saw, behind Dr Azarian, Cara perched on a stool.

"Isn't this private?" Liza asked.

"Oh, she won't *look*," he said.

Cara was not wearing the headset, which rested on her knee. In a pale-green linen shirt, jeans, and heels, she looked as if she should be on a patio sipping a drink, in the ether with Angeline's holographic self. Cara's face was floodlit by the lamp beside Liza's head, her hair glowing red, her smile more significant in the glare. Bobby stood to one side, looking at a pad of paper. He produced a pen from his pocket, flourished it.

"How are you feeling?" Cara asked.

"Fine. Just fine. Dr Azarian?"

"You should call him Bobby. She should call you Bobby."

"Call me Bobby."

"Why is she here?"

"She wants to know why you're here," Bobby said, his pen moving in a way that made Liza guess he was doodling.

"I want to ask you some questions," Cara said, as if that was enough of an answer.

"Can I get up?"

Cara touched the metal edge of the table by Liza's head. "Not yet."

At first, Cara asked dinner party questions: how she met Neal, where she worked before, if she had grown up in the city. It was nice for someone to ask her something. So she let herself be nudged towards childhood, favourite books or films or colours, dead cats and birds. Then slowly towards the smaller, more elusive things, things she hadn't considered in years. The metallic tang of the tap water in her grandmother's house, her feet burning through her sandals, standing in the driveway, the dust lifting in the street, the shapes the dust made delighting her, too young at five to know it was a sign of the Great Drought. The water sluiced back into her throat. Cara stroked her forehead; she barely minded, recalling the water.

There was another sound in the room now too, a hum. It reminded her of the hum of an old space heater. The room was so warm.

"I'm recording you," Cara said. "I hope you don't mind."

"I don't mind." The warmth made it difficult to think.

"Thank you," said Angeline from the headset on Cara's knee, her voice small and far away. Cara had a notebook balanced on her other knee and was taking notes in tiny, constrained cursive.

"It's to match the recording," Cara said, "part of building the full picture. I know it's kind of affected, to write things down, but I like it. I've accepted it as part of my process."

"Don't be afraid," Angeline said from the headset.

"Change is good," Bobby added, clicking his pen shut, pulling a face so they would know he was making fun of them, of himself, that nothing was serious, not even this.

"Show her," Cara said.

He held up the paper. There was Liza, on the table, suggested by a few ink strokes. But her face was rendered in precise and loving detail, pensive, naked, without the self-correction of mirrors and photographs. She hadn't known she looked like that.

"Can I keep it?"

"Of course, it's for you," Cara said.

"Thank you," Angeline said again, as Bobby folded the drawing into a square, placed it on Liza's open palm.

She was so heavy. It was different than the heaviness before sleep, more like the way her hands or feet felt when the circulation was cut off by staying in one position too long.

Leaden, tingling. And then something else beginning, a fluttering inside her that was like panic, but not her panic. Like she could feel a bird buffeting inside her chest.

She closed her eyes again. And heard a voice, a familiar soothing voice, telling other stories, memories as intimate and commonplace as her own. But the voice was inside her now. Whispering tenderly inside her thoughts. She was sure that if she spoke, her voice would have become two voices, braided together like the harmony in a song. She didn't speak. She was too tired to speak. The fluttering was easing now. But what she'd felt inside her was growing. Unfurling in her brain and her blood. Stretching tendrils, rejoicing in the space that was inside her. Strong as a plant finding the sun.

She didn't try to move from the table. She knew the door was sealed, and anyway, there was Cara and Sally with her helpful idea and Neal hammering on the door and she knew now why they had brought her here.

"You're doing great. I'm so, so proud of you," Cara said, and Liza couldn't tell which one of them she was speaking to. Both.

She wondered what it would feel like when the transition was fully accomplished. If there would be a moment when she and Angeline would consciously inhabit her body at the same time, and after that, where she would go. She was sure they had prepared a place for her. Maybe she would be given Angeline's beautiful bare room.

Travellers

THE CAR LURCHED IN LATE AFTERNOON TRAFFIC. Trout's palms were stuck to the seat. The driver frowned into the mirror, talking into his earpiece; she couldn't tell if he was unsure of her expression or displeased by his conversation. The highway was flanked by condo towers, then warehouses, then the grey-and-black rectangles of business-traveller hotels. Beyond the shoulder, flashes of short stiff grass.

At the airport, she searched the screen for her flight, counting her breaths. Her suitcase listed on its broken wheel as she dragged it to her gate.

Step onto this walkway.

Into this line.

Through this sliding door.

Lift your arms.

Take off your shoes.

Take off your watch.

Relinquish your wallet and your passport to a series of strangers.

The airport was a mysterious city. The openness was an illusion, the terminal was full of unseen corridors, suitcases moving along interlocking plates through tunnels, then tumbling into vast plastic bins, transformed, when separated from their owners, into something potentially threatening. Towers, searchlights, painted lines. The implausible lift of the plane itself. The brightness and the glass and steel and gleaming plastic all seemed like empty reassurance, a promise that she must be a fool to believe in. It made no sense to believe in it. She would have to believe in it. She counted her breaths.

Standing in the security line, Trout looked around her, wondering if anyone else was resisting an urge to make a sudden movement or scream or run. Like waiting for the subway and wanting to leap into the path of the train, not from wishing to die, not anything so final, more from a startled moment of perceiving her own obedience as arbitrary. Terror but also freedom. She hoped this journey might unlock her, wasn't that the purpose of a journey?

Trout was going to visit her friend Strawberry in Berlin, and considering leaving her husband Tim, though she had not yet admitted this to anyone; the trip was partly a thought experiment, an opportunity to pretend she had already left. Tim didn't know Strawberry well, and had met her only once, when she had shown up at their apartment in Toronto more or less unannounced ten years earlier and stayed for three weeks. He hadn't spoken much in her presence, though Trout suspected he was privately peeved by Strawberry's failure to notice the things other women admired: his self-effacement, his attention to the housework, his demonstrations of regard for Trout's time and opinions. Whether or not a man gave equitable notice to a woman did not interest Strawberry. She talked mostly to Trout, mixed drinks that slopped from their glasses, spit over the railing of the back deck onto the grass, wiped her mouth on her sleeve. She referred to Tim as *your husband* with mock solemnity, as though a husband was a silly thing to have. After she left, Tim had pointed out the track marks along Strawberry's left arm; Trout hadn't even noticed. He asked that Strawberry not stay with them again, which was one of Trout's first glimpses into a kind of lack in him. He told Trout she was naive, but she thought that he was naive in a different way, with his demands for appropriate boundaries, his limited sense of what was acceptable. He was right, of course. She was naive. But she would rather be naive than cruel.

Trout and Strawberry had been born in the same week, in the same commune, into a world that smelled of mildew and dope, of compost and rubber boots, wet wool and sacks of weevilled flour, still used for bread, money being meagre. Trout's mother had hemorrhaged and been driven to the nearest hospital down potholed country roads in the dawn. Trout's first milk had come from Strawberry's mother, who'd sworn the two babies held hands, reaching across her heavily veined breasts. Trout didn't believe that anymore. So much of their life in that place had relied on signs that sometimes the signs had to be fabricated, to shore up their strenuous dedication. Trout's mother had been pronounced malnourished and sent back home, where she had eaten tofu and drunk the last of the goat's milk, sitting hip to hip with Strawberry's mother in the old loveseat on the farmhouse porch, the two babies dressed in threadbare sleepers, yellow paint daubed on their bulging foreheads to represent the opening of the third eye.

When Trout was ten, her mother had left, stealing one of the old cars. Trout remembered the fried eggs that her mother bought her when they stopped at a roadside motel, but she couldn't remember if she'd known they were leaving for good. Her mother cleaned houses in Toronto, cut her hair, cut Trout's, eventually got a job as a receptionist, wearing large blue glasses, her feet slung into chunky high-heeled shoes. She adopted an ironic flirtatiousness in her dealings with what Trout thought of as the hostile world, which made Trout feel that this new life was not quite safe, it was so at odds with who her mother had been. Barefoot, unsmiling. A person incapable of capitulation. Trout, reluctantly enrolled in the local school where she stood at recess with her hands wound through the chain-link fence, would let herself into their basement apartment in the afternoons and draw at the table until her mother came home. Her mother used to steal coloured pens and paper from the office where she worked, lifting them out of her bag and passing them to Trout conspiratorially.

Strawberry and her parents remained, stubborn in their voluntary poverty, or too stunted to imagine an elsewhere. She secretly wrote letters to Trout in Toronto and Trout wrote back, sending her letters to the post office in the town, where they were collected by Strawberry's mother, breaking a no-contact pronouncement out of love for her child and telling no one, not even Strawberry's father. Strawberry's letters were effusive, Trout's restrained. She could not tell Strawberry she missed her even once. It would be like telling her mother how unhappy she was.

When Strawberry turned eighteen, she stole all the money from the tin on the farmhouse fridge, walked into town, and bought a bus ticket to Pittsburgh, where she found her grand-parents, who had not heard from their daughter in twenty years. She sent a letter to her parents saying she wouldn't be returning, got a job as a waitress, saved money for an adventure that would kick-start the rest of her life, and flipped a coin between New York and Berlin. Her grandparents helped her get a passport, she found her people in a squat in Prenzlberg and became the lover of a well-known artist twenty years her senior who gave her heroin and paint. The artist overdosed, cementing his reputation, and her status in his life launched hers just enough for her to remain in view, find buyers, get clean eventually, give eccentric and sometimes brash interviews that hinted at a depth of childhood catastrophe beyond anything Trout felt either of them had actually experienced.

She tried to give Strawberry the benefit of the doubt: chil-dren hide things, though it seemed to her equally true that adults, reflecting on childhood, allow themselves to make a story that follows the rules of stories for and about children, with clear villains, clear central characters, a direct line between cause and effect, creating a framework that will explain their dissatis-factions. Strawberry was her own material. Her subject, officially, was fairy tales (a battered copy of the Brothers Grimm being one of the books the children in the farmhouse were allowed to read), her first success an installation of raw pig gut looped with human hair: the female body, the umbilical cord. The gut grew iridescent, decayed slowly in a glass case with round openings through which the spectators could smell. This was followed by a series using dolls, with keys or branches for hair, casts of open mouths with knives for teeth, in one (Trout had leaned into the image Strawberry sent her, fascinated), a tiny boat poised on the doll's jabbing tongue, which was made from a wooden ice cream spoon. The boat held a pinhead-sized child of blown glass, clinging to the prow. Strawberry then moved to paintings, always sending Trout the exhibition catalogue afterwards. The girls in the paintings were not generic: Trout recognized Strawberry's face, and her own. Girls in bloody slips, behind which indeterminate figures loomed. Odd dashes of white like birds or ghosts above their heads. Though suspicious, Trout conceded to the force of the paintings. What could have been posturing had the potency of songs, of authorless stories. *My mother she killed me, my father he ate me.*

In Berlin, Strawberry used a roster of names. Fictional girls: Matilda, Pippi, Madeleine, appearing as illuminated signatures in the corners of her paintings. Only Trout still called her Strawberry. Her work, grown a little old-fashioned, was still successful enough for her to support herself from it. She was upholstered in fabric, her body thin and plucked of all hair, except complicated knots and shaved patterns on her head. A tree of life, tattooed along her back, sent roots winding down her legs, branches disappearing into her hairline. The red birthmark over her left eye that had inspired her original name was accented by brown eyeshadow. Trout sought out her photograph, which accompanied the profiles that occasionally appeared in art magazines or on websites. Strawberry didn't smile in the photographs, as if she didn't want to risk exposure, though she often appeared naked, her arms crossed over her breasts, her face expressionless as plaster.

On the plane, Trout sat very straight, waiting for the first streaks of light to appear. She'd fallen out of a tree, the year they left, and broken her leg, which sometimes twinged, especially when she travelled. John, the leader of the commune, older than most of the other members and at that point rewriting the Bible, was in a new phase in which doctors were Pharisees who did not understand Primal Love, and so he visualized healing over her leg while the bone set itself, knit together. She walked with an almost imperceptible limp.

Trout's husband was an actor, and he had that absorbent quality that genuinely talented actors have, always watching for what the other person wanted, adjusting himself to this want. This had been wonderful for a while, and so different from what she thought of as the fanaticism, the rigidity, that she and Strawberry were born into and had escaped. But now, lying awake beside Tim at night, she thought she had gone too far the other way, that his talent and his good nature obscured smugness, a lack of curiosity. He was not graspable. She had not grasped him. Perhaps she didn't know how to demand anything; her life with her mother had not prepared her to make demands.

Trout had been married for fifteen years. They had no children, though children had been at times talked about and she didn't really think of herself as a childless person, more that she was still waiting for her life to begin, even as she knew, practically speaking, that it was half-over.

She borrowed money from her half-brother, who was fourteen years younger and a real estate agent in Vancouver and paid their mother's bills, and bought herself a ticket to Berlin, thinking that Strawberry, with all her cataclysms, knew, in a way Trout had refused to know, that life was not only casual or provisional, and that to believe that led to the kind of uncertain sorrow that Trout now found herself in.

A few years after Strawberry left, John had gone for a walk and been found two weeks later, both legs twisted under him at the bottom of a stony gully. Foxes and crows had eaten his eyes and tongue and part of one of his ears. Without him, the commune dwindled to only a few people. John had anchored them. He had claimed he'd had a vision in the desert as a young man, just after the Second World War, in which the life they shared came to him whole, in every detail. Trout thought that he'd been a mixture of conman and madman, promising a future that he almost believed in, enough to make other people believe, if they were sufficiently adrift. As a child, she had loved the singing and dancing, the penitential rituals and occasional feast days, cribbed from whatever tradition happened to take John's fancy and made over to suit his rickety cosmology. She remembered her early life, even as she'd rejected it, as a happiness that nothing afterwards had matched.

Trout's mother had early-onset dementia and was in an assisted living facility. Trout visited her every second day, biking from the theatre where she managed the box office, sitting with her mother as the light faded, helping her eat dinner. Her mother moved the food around her mouth, exploring it with her tongue, and needed to be reminded to swallow. Trout had suffered some pangs as she planned this escape to see Strawberry, but comforted herself with the thought that Naomi would probably not notice she was gone. Her mother had become a person outside time, or at least outside chronological time.

"Excuse me?"

A young man stood in front of her; she'd been looking down at her phone. She nearly ran into him. She'd waited in the arrivals area at Tegel airport for nearly an hour, calling Strawberry over and over with no answer. She had an address but no directions, and her phone was dying. Her charger was somewhere in the depths of her suitcase. She couldn't see any payphones. A patrolling security guard shrugged when asked for directions. She wanted to feel she was entering one of the great cities of the world, a place in which her life would become clear. But the airport was shabby, with gummy cracks in the concrete floor, and she was an exhausted middle-aged woman in danger of crying in public.

"Is it possible to help? You are lost?"

He was not German, she thought, and spoke English diffidently, as though she might reprove him. Perhaps she was unmistakably North American. Perhaps she'd been talking to herself. She looked around. The corridor was full of movement;

she and the man were the only people standing still. He was young, in jeans and a pleated wool cardigan, his face obscured by a soft fall of brown hair and large silver-rimmed glasses. She imagined that if she pressed his cheek her thumb would leave a print, a small hollow.

"Is it possible to help?" he asked again.

She showed him the address, smiling apologetically. He peered at it, his hair hiding his eyes.

"Yes," he said, pleased, "I know it. I know it."

He handed the dying phone back. She didn't know if she was supposed to say anything.

"I've never been here before," she offered.

"This is near where I am going myself. I will take you there. Come."

She protested. He kept smiling. She followed him outside. They stood side by side in the line for the bus. On the bus, he led her to the upper level at the back, directed her to sit by the window.

"Now you may see where we are going," he said. It was raining. The highways around the airport gave way to the city itself, concrete ridges of office buildings, interludes of parks and public lawns, monuments. The streets became more crowded with people, more blotched with advertisements. Everywhere she looked she saw construction, orange cranes, cobblestones crowning piles of wet sand. The young man also looked out the window, his hands in his lap. He had no suitcase, only a small bag over his shoulder. She asked him where he was coming from. He was coming from Tartu, he said, in Estonia, where he

had studied mathematics. He lived in Berlin now and wished
to be a travel journalist. Once she had asked her single question,
he talked freely. He had gone home because his mother was
unwell. She did not live in the city, he explained (Trout did not
know that Tartu was a city), cities made his mother too anxious,
and she had not visited him his entire time at university. He
went home to her, where she lived in a small cabin in the woods,
near the village where she had grown up. It was just the two of
them, he said, his voice dropping as though this was a delicate
matter, the two of them in the house in the woods. His father
had been killed when his car went off the road before he himself was born, and Trout, who could not remember her father,
caught the shame in this, laughter directed at the small boy by
older boys, not old enough to want to be kind. He had never
been to school before he left for Tartu, he said, and Trout was
startled, thinking of herself, of woods, of tramping through the
leaves. Maybe he was an angel. She had been taught to believe
in angels. Maybe she'd met one at last. He had a lesson plan,
he went on, which the school board sent, and which he com-
pleted on the computer. His heart was weak, he was frightened,
his mother kept him home. The huge stone buildings of the
University of Tartu were a shock to him. His life had not prepared him for anything larger than the clock tower in the town
where they bought groceries. He stood with his hopeful little
bag, dazzled by the lampposts, the faces of the other students.
His first year, he said, smiling at the bus window, he almost
never spoke. But now he wanted to go far, to see places and
write about them. She didn't ask how he intended to become

a travel journalist or why he had chosen Berlin. She imagined him in a small, scrupulously clean single room with a hotplate, eating bread and jam, soup from a can, spooned methodically into his mouth as he tried to write.

She followed him off the bus, down into the U-Bahn. He walked directly in front of her, shielding her from the crowd.

"See," he said, pointing to the map on the wall in the corridor, "it is simple from here. This line, and down. We will go together. I will walk you to the apartment of your friend."

She demurred.

"I am not troubled. It is not trouble."

It was louder on the train. He stopped talking, as if he had said all he needed her to know.

She wouldn't let him take her suitcase up the stairs. She could see that he was hurt, as though she feared he might run off into the crowd. He walked more quickly and she thought he would vanish. But he was waiting at the top of the stairs, watching her struggle. She wanted to explain that she trusted him and then was aggravated that he would think she owed him trust. The whole episode was unnecessary. She could have found an info kiosk at the airport, she could have unpacked her charger and kept calling Strawberry, she didn't know what had made her decide to follow him, she did not need to protect his feelings.

"Come now, come," he said when she reached him, and patted her knuckles, whitened around the handle of her suitcase. It was a kindness, to touch her hand like that. She had been ungenerous. She would never see him again. About to thank him, she heard her name called.

"Oh fuck. Oh fuck me. I'm such an asshole. I thought it was p.m. I was just going to get us food. I lost my phone somewhere yesterday."

Strawberry kissed Trout elaborately on her forehead, cheeks, and the tip of her nose. Trout was caught off guard by how drawn she was, more than had been evident from the pixelated blur of Trout's old laptop. Her neck was ropy, and spicy oils came off her skin. Her hair was dyed canary yellow, and she had a new vine tattoo starting behind her left ear and down across her shoulder, which was bare except for the strap of her purple dress. Her broad face was pallid, sunless, with slashes of pinkish-bronze powder on her cheeks, her mouth painted almost white. She grinned, showing her crooked teeth, inflamed gums. Trout turned in Strawberry's arms, looking for the boy, but he was gone.

She tried to describe him, waving her free hand, trailing Strawberry through the grocery store, her suitcase squeaking on the shiny tiles. Strawberry, not interested, produced string bags from her pockets (*look at me, such a hausfrau*), picked out fruit, dark bread.

"And meat! Meat! We'll get everything. To honour the soy years."

She pointed at marbled and swirled cold cuts, speaking in heavily accented German that made the man behind the counter switch to English, selected wedges of cheese, orange juice, cake, glass jars of milk and yogurt. She swung the bags in front of her as they reached the street.

"We'll walk," she said. "I want to show you where I live."

There was green paint under her nails, blue on her collarbone. Trout knew she was working towards a solo show, three months away; Trout would be expected to see the paintings, was already preparing the mixture of praise and confusion that Strawberry seemed to require. She hoped she was up to it.

Four lanes of traffic sailed by, and Trout kept veering off the paved part of the sidewalk and towards the outer cobbles, the bells of speeding bikes trilling at her. Strawberry stopped walking and lit a cigarette.

"That's my favourite bar, I'll take you there tonight," aiming her foot at a building with shuttered windows, lettering faded to pink on a white sign, a handwritten message on a wrinkled piece of paper covering the pebbled glass portal of the door. "That says the bathrooms are only for customers. You'll love it, it's such a holdout, it's got sawdust on the floor and it's full of sweaty Germans who don't speak English and don't talk to me. I don't know where these dirty old guys come from, this neighbourhood is totally spick-and-span now, but they still show up here, these guys, get pissed out of their minds. I used to think they were Nazis but the Nazis are dead with cute little grave markers, I can show you those too, these guys lived through the Soviets, though, tough fuckers, *real* Berliners."

Trout couldn't tell what made the people walking past them unreal Berliners. Strawberry moved on, Trout struggled after her.

"The gentrification is insane, there was nothing like that when I came here, it's sad this is the first time you're seeing it. Look, just look! So *clean*, so nice-nice. I think it's a plot to make all the cities in the world look like the same city, not even for tourists, this isn't for tourists, these aren't tourists, for people who live here so they can think they live anywhere. And everybody is so uptight! Tilting to the right like everywhere else, well, not Berlin, but maybe it's just more subtle, having everything cleaned up is the thin end of the wedge."

Trout, her spirits rising at the unfamiliarity of the street and the people, couldn't see how this city was like any other city. She thought it was more difficult than that, to bleach out the particularity of a place, even if Strawberry had a right to her prissy nostalgia for what must have felt like her best times, when she was a precarious and avaricious young woman, sprawled in the mess of the former East, her eyes widening *yes* at anything on offer: art, sex, needles, history lessons. The world so much larger than she'd thought.

They turned down a side street lined with low-rise apartments, old stone abutting stucco, grafted together like repair on a ravaged mouth.

"Hurry up," Strawberry said, "we're just up here. I'm kind of street shy, don't go out much. I get jumpy."

She swung her bags jauntily, and one of them hit a pole. Glass cracked, yogurt belched through the netting.

"It's okay. I bought two."

She ignored a white spatter behind her and they stopped in front of one of the grey buildings. She cursed, searching for her key. Pigeons complained from the ledges.

"This is like the last un-renovated building in the city. I had to sleep with the landlord, practically. It's all drywall and security codes now. I'm never leaving, they'll carry me out."

Trout followed Strawberry through the dirty lobby, the plaster pitted and the stone stairs chipped, and climbed to the fourth floor, passing by leaded windows as large as doors on each landing, which looked out onto scaffolding and a shared courtyard. On the third landing, Trout could hear a woman in one of the apartments losing her temper. The open door showed a long hallway, shoe rack, navy-blue baby stroller, coats hanging on carved pegs, kitchen shining whitely at the end. The neat apartment made the seediness of the building seem superficial, one of Strawberry's self-aggrandizing pronouncements.

Strawberry led her up the final flight of stairs, prodded her through the door. Trout stood in the gloom as Strawberry kicked her suitcase to one side, put the leaking bag in the sink, mopped up the trail she'd left, only as far as the threshold, ignoring the drips in the hallway.

The apartment was smaller than the one below, though with very high ceilings, and still big enough that Trout could imagine running across it, towards windows that led to a small concrete platform with no railing. Several terracotta pots, empty except for dry earth, lined its edge. One large room, nearly unfurnished, broad floorboards splashed with paint. A small table in the centre, crowded with metal chairs. A mattress was wedged onto a wooden platform with a ladder up to it, and a second mattress, made up with touching precision, lay on the floor underneath. A couch, a few crates of books crowded overtop with scarves, junky ornaments, hardened spills of coloured wax. Fridge, sink, warped plywood counter along one wall. A folding door to a wobbly toilet and shower.

Covered canvases sat on easels or leaned against the walls. Ranging from taller than Trout down to the size of a portrait photograph, they gave the room the feeling of an abandoned factory. Or not abandoned, suspended for Trout's entrance; she could feel the tension in Strawberry, the way she tried not to notice whether Trout appeared fittingly curious. Strawberry, turning away, smacked at a row of light switches. Trout touched one of the plastic sheets, which was ragged, paint-splattered.

"Don't you dare. Those are for later," Strawberry said over her shoulder, chopping fruit. She nicked her finger and stuck it under the tap. She must have covered them for Trout's arrival.

Trout slept after they ate, still in her clothes under the duvet. It was late afternoon when she woke, and the windows streamed weak sunshine. She sat up, knowing that she'd dreamed of the young man, not remembering what. Passageways and doors, leaves scudding along a street, a figure in the woods. In the shower, she scrubbed herself with expensive-smelling brown gels, gritty against her skin. Wrapping herself in Strawberry's somewhat dank yellow towel, she walked to one of the paintings. Something red swirled underneath the sheet, and an uncovered corner showed a disc of blackened silver like an old coin. The latch clicked behind her.

"I got some wine," Strawberry said. "I was going to take you out, but I don't want to. We'll eat here. Stay in the towel if you want, I'll crank the heat, it's fucking freezing outside."

Trout dressed.

Strawberry set the wine on the table. "I didn't get more food, can we just finish the lunch stuff?" she asked, already taking the containers back out of the fridge.

Trout pulled socks over her damp feet.

"I'm glad you're here," Strawberry said, sounding surprised, drawing out two cigarettes and lighting them, handing one to Trout. They smoked, each wondering what the next two weeks would be like. With one hand, Strawberry fanned meat and cheese onto a cutting board, opened older Styrofoam containers full of hummus, olives, whitish slices of tomatoes, adeptly making the table beautiful, flicking a lighter and dipping it at a candle. The lights were off again, except for tangled strings of Edison bulbs running along the floor by one wall. The candle flame sharpened Strawberry's face, and Trout wondered how long it had been since someone had sat with her at this table. Strawberry did not eat, drank wine from a mug, which left a dark stain on her mouth. She pulled a flap of skin from her lip, rolled it into a ball between her fingers. The curator was an asshole, this or that friend had been lost to domesticity, her rent was going up, the landlord was thinking of selling the building, she'd broken up with the woman she'd been seeing, again. Trout saw no need to answer. Strawberry must often talk to herself, working alone in this big cold room. Strawberry refilled her mug, tipped two inches into Trout's. She had somehow worked herself onto the Baader-Meinhof Gang, lit another cigarette, inhaled clumsily, coughed on the smoke. Her skin tight across her forehead, slack at the chin, her eyes watering, her bravado stopped short. Trout, light-headed from the cigarette (she hadn't smoked in years), had a panicked impulse to text her husband that she loved him. But she couldn't remember where she'd put her phone. She didn't get up. She sinned in her heart.

Sinning in your heart was a frequent accusation at the commune, meaning some kind of untenable ambivalence, a failure of courage. Trout's mother was often accused and had to stand in the middle of the circle while each member stepped forward and enumerated her failings, and she wore a stern, patient expression that Trout admired and wanted to imitate.

Children were not included in this circle but gathered to watch outside it. Trout didn't understand why her mother sinned in her heart: she was a hard worker, she did anything John asked without asking why. Then, when Trout was lifted out of her bed and carried to the car, she thought they must have been right, and her mother was not brave enough. Sometimes, in the care facility, Trout's mother would berate, in scraps and unfinished sentences, Strawberry's mother, and Trout would hold her breath, hoping for more; there was so much she had never asked about, believing that she preferred not to know, and now, when she was no longer sure that was true, it was too late for questions.

"Did you know that one of the old Baader-Meinhof guys is a Nazi now, they keep him in prison because they just can't risk releasing him, and all he does is write about the purity of the German race and the Jewish threat? It's true, it's *true*, I read about it. I want to paint him. I'd like to get permission to paint him. I'm really interested in the number of artists who were attracted to fascism because they thought it was strong. You know. Virile. It makes for terrible artists, terrible art, can't produce anything except kitsch, it's like the Soviets and socialist realism, that's what you get when you have a totally stable and ideologically fixed conception of social relationships, you can't actually make art anymore, you've cut yourself off. But at the beginning, all these artists really flirted with it, I guess they thought it was the next big thing. It fascinates me how that's coming back. I know *fascist* gets thrown around a lot these days to mean anything you don't agree with, but sometimes a fascist is really a fascist. I want to make a series of paintings after this one, something about that. I used to like watching Milo Yiannopoulos on YouTube—"

"Jesus Christ," Trout said, supplying the expected reaction but also meaning it, "that—"

"Exactly, he's like staring into the void. He's puerile and he's not dangerous—"

"Yes he is—"

"Don't be such a goody two-shoes, I'm not finished, he's not dangerous and attractive because he believes hateful things, he's dangerous and attractive—don't make that face, not to me—he's dangerous and attractive because it looks to me like he believes *nothing*. I can't figure him out. It's like watching a performance art project and you can't tell what's satire and what's serious because the distinction might not matter. I don't think he knows anymore, if he ever did, he just hit a nerve and he likes hitting a nerve. Turns out a lot of people want to be told they can love power because it's power and seek it because it's there. Whoops! We miscalculated! It turns out we just want the void."

"Don't watch people like that. You'll get lost."

"Oh my darling. Oh honey. I *am* lost."

Trout pictured Strawberry in front of the screen late at night, cigarette smoke gathered around her head like a thought bubble, no one coming home, no one telling her to come to bed, to think about something else. Trout wondered again where she'd put her phone.

"Maybe I like it because it's so different from my parents, but in another way not at all. They wanted to tear everything down too. Fuck. Or that's not right. They wanted to tell everybody else how to live. They were so *sanctimonious* about it. I get so angry when I think about that generation. You know, born after, will die before."

"What?"

"You *know*," Strawberry said tetchily, shaking her head, appealing to a shorthand Trout wasn't aware they had, "born after, died before. Born after the war, dying before the shit hits the fan. We are the last generation on earth that's going to get old. We're burning up."

"*Our work is guided by the sense that we might be the last generation in the experiment with living,*" Trout quoted.

"What's that?"

"The Port Huron Statement. Your dad put it up in the kitchen, remember?"

"I forgot! That's funny I forgot. You know, I used to think I'd never get out alive. By the time I left, I thought he would lose it some night and think he was a prophet and soak us in gas. I was walking to town to go to the library by then. I knew about Jonestown. He was an okay father, sometimes, but I thought that was how we'd finish up. Just a fireball going up to the sky. When I got to Pittsburgh it was the most beautiful thing

I'd ever seen, this sad, collapsed city. I got off the bus and my eyes stung, you never told me that, how your eyes sting when you aren't used to pollution. When you live in the middle of nowhere in Maine. I wanted everything, everything, I wanted to get in a fight with someone, I wanted to get mugged! I wanted to break somebody's nose! I just wanted everything that could happen to a person to happen to me."

She stroked Trout's palm absently across the table, and Trout closed her hand over Strawberry's. Strawberry gripped hard and then withdrew, leaning back in her chair with her chin tilted at the ceiling.

"I keep having these dreams," she said, quieter now, "where airplanes fall out of the sky because the world is ending. It's final and calm, these huge airbuses falling. First it's just one and I think, okay. That's okay, one we can handle, one we can recover from. Even though I hate myself for thinking that, but then more and more fall, turning over in the air and landing in this field, I'm standing in the field, it's marshy with a few trees. Small trees, maybe thorn trees, you know, small. And then I told some people about the dream and it turns out I'm not the only person having the dream. So I knew it was a sign. You know, maybe they were right, when they told us we had to pay attention to signs."

She closed her eyes, moved by her own narration. Trout thought of the young man, somewhere in this city, and that he was a sign, but she didn't know what of and couldn't explain this to Strawberry, who was only interested in her own signs, signs that had to have a fairly obvious meaning. Trout didn't know what he meant. Was he required, as an angel, to mean anything? She imagined going out, down into the street, searching, finding him. Outlined in light from a window, holding his little soup spoon. She didn't know what she would say or ask. Strawberry remained silent and Trout wondered at what she'd hinted at through all those imperilled little girls, and whether she resented Trout for having been rescued by her mother. For having a mother who'd opted for the compromised and the commonplace, for traffic lights and dental plans and the illusion of safety. She thought of her mother in her chair, tended by nurses, and Tim, whom she might or might not leave, and Strawberry unnerved her enough to remind her how good it could be, how sweet, to have someone who prevented her from being alone with her own thoughts. She wondered if Strawberry not only resented her but had a right to, if she owed Strawberry some question or acknowledgement that she had never given her. Even with her modest, frozen life, she had been rescued and Strawberry had not. No one had cared to rescue her.

Trout wanted to say all this and didn't. She was not good at asking questions, at saying what she thought; she so rarely knew what she thought. She tentatively reached for Strawberry's hand again, and Strawberry moved her hand away.

Somewhere, down below, the young man was eating his soup.

Strawberry got up, stretched.

"Come on," she said, "I'm going to show you."

She made Trout stand in the centre of the room and close her eyes. Reddish darkness, grown brighter as a lamp was switched on. With her eyes shut, the room grew. She heard the hiss and

soft scratch of a plastic sheet being carefully pulled away, the
rustle as Strawberry dragged it across the floor, tucked it into
a corner. Pauses, Strawberry's concentrated breath as the sheet
caught on canvas corners or the edges of chairs.

"Okay, you can look," Strawberry said.

She'd uncovered only the largest, which was beside the
window. It was a triptych, set on hinges. The standing lamp
beside it was trained to the floor, so that the light didn't hit
the images directly. Strawberry was already talking at her, near
her left ear, about influence, about Hieronymus Bosch and
photographs of repossessed houses in Texas and Christopher
Wood's paintings of houses and Kristeva's writing on female
defilement and how she'd used her own blood as a pigment
which was what that shade of brown was and how the root of
the word *haunted* was the Old Norse *heimta*, to bring home,
to fetch, and Trout wished she would stop even if Strawberry
was talking in order to pretend that Trout didn't frighten her
as much as she frightened Trout, as the only person still in her
life who could remember what she remembered, contradict it,
correct it, magnify it. Hearing Strawberry monologuing, she
thought, with guilt and guilty satisfaction, that she was still the
person Strawberry most wanted to give an account of herself
to, the person whose judgment she most feared. Trout knew
that she shouldn't find this so gratifying, but she did. It helped
her feel she really existed.

The central image was Trout's mother, standing in the middle of the circle, the faces around her contorted in accusation,
but their rage was not satisfying to them. It looked like pain.
Trout's mother was wearing a white dress, a wreath of blue

flowers, and an expression Trout did not remember from that time but recognized from her mother's present face. Muddled, like a faithful kicked dog. As if she had been forced out, instead of deciding to go. As if she had begged to stay. Maybe Strawberry had seen that then, and remembered it. Maybe Strawberry had been told that. Maybe the people who remained wished that had been true, although, looking at her mother's face in the picture, Trout went a step further and thought that Strawberry had seen something that was true, if not literally, something Trout had missed completely, willfully, the hurt in that face, the sincerity. She had thought of Strawberry as seeing only herself, but there in the picture was Trout's mother: someone who could be forgiven, or at least understood, and Trout (she didn't want this feeling, she wanted it to stop now) had not tried to do either, not enough.

To the left was the car, leaving, with Trout's ten-year-old face pressed to the back window but drawn blank, a pale oval like a hole. In this imagining, a horde of people followed them, carrying shovels, pitchforks, torches, guns. Each person their own recognizable self, even though some of them had been rendered as animals: roosters, goats, pigs. Trout wondered how many of them were dead, or coughing softly in rooming houses or prison cells, or whether, like her mother, they had eventually found their way back to repudiated families, to flush toilets and clocks.

Then she saw the figure standing in the path of the car, arms stretched out, barely sketched, with the road and the pricking stars visible through the torso. It was Strawberry as a child, barefoot, wearing a ripped T-shirt and no pants, rescuing Trout. She would stop the car and drag Trout back and keep her so they would have the same memories and the same secrets and the same futures, as if it were possible to continue as they had been, as Trout, recalling, could feel in her stomach with the force of an unexpected blow. Strawberry's breath on her face, their arms and legs tangled together, sleeping in piles of hay in the henhouse, each of them making do with each other as protector and second self.

The picture to the right was, like Trout leaving in the car, something Strawberry had never seen, only heard about, and Trout couldn't tell whether she was angry at the presumption or amazed at how closely Strawberry must have listened, even when she seemed incapable of paying attention. Trout's mother sitting up in her reclining chair, with her attendants thrusting objects (tubes, food trays, charts) at her that she didn't want and was not allowed to refuse. Hieronymus Bosch made sense: this was a vision of hell, teeming and endless, punishment for whatever her sins might be. She was wearing a pale-blue hospital gown and matching high heels, the kind of shoes she hadn't worn for years and had never worn well, work shoes, kicked off with a theatrical sigh when she came back to the basement apartment where Trout was stirring the soup she'd heated from a tin, after drawing two girls that she'd tacked on the wall with the other drawings, though when they moved in with the man who was briefly Trout's stepfather her mother threw the pictures away, hoping, as she always had, for a new start.

Strawberry had finally stopped talking, looking at Trout. Trout, who was weeping, found it difficult to interpret her mother's face in this last picture, since both her hands were clamped over her mouth.

Pilgrims

I walk in the footsteps of Saint Francis. Like him, I talk with animals. Birds fly near me. I could climb mountains.

The screen glowed white-blue; the rest of the room was dark. He coughed in the bedroom behind her. She could hear moths beating against the door of the trailer. She coughed back: I'm here.

—

She posted a photograph of a road in Spain.

My name is Sister Bernadette. I am a Franciscan Nun, originally from Wisconsin, where my order is based. I am now living in Northumberland County, on a special dispensation to leave the order so that I can take care of my brother, who is a quadriplegic. I have started this blog so I can share my thoughts on the spiritual life, and to establish connections with others in the Christian Community.

I live simply, even away from the order, in keeping with my vows. My life is one of prayer and contemplation. Most of my time is taken up with looking after my brother, and his example of patient suffering helps me to follow in the path of Christ.

My dream is to walk the Camino. I tell myself that what I am walking is my private Camino, and that the Lord sees my steps, as much as He sees the footprints of the pilgrims. But, being human, I struggle to reconcile myself to God's will.

Brother sounded better than son or stepson. She knew it was possible for a nun to have children, if she'd joined later in life, but how could you be a real nun and have children? A nun was supposed to be special, untouched by the world, untouched. And Stevie was something that came with Nickel, and that Nickel had left behind. "We're a package deal," Nickel told her, when Stevie was five, with darkening hair and a nose-picking habit. Now he was a nineteen-year-old who'd flown through a windshield, and Nickel had decided this wasn't his package. Well, men decide that sometimes, and still forgive themselves, even when nobody else does. She lit a cigarette, blew the smoke at the screen, watched it disperse in the close room.

—

Her mother used to listen to Jennifer Warnes sing "The Song of Bernadette" and cry. It was embarrassing; her mother would cry anywhere. At commercials, in the supermarket, like it was nothing. But it was a nice name, nicer than hers. She didn't know why her mother didn't name her Bernadette.

—

The trailer was large and damp: two bedrooms, a kitchenette, a bathroom, a living room. When she moved into it, Nickel had not said anything about something temporary, had been proud as a child. It was something she loved about him. This was his home, his land. He painted and read and dealt pot with single-minded contentment, his long skinny body stooping unconsciously in the low doorways. She supposed it was the single-mindedness that had made him so attractive in his self-sufficiency, a self-sufficiency that made it possible for him to leave her and Stevie, a year ago now. He was merciless. It was what made him appear so happy.

The trailer had sunk into the landscape. The wheels were inches deep in the ground, softening in the spring thaw, then hardening as the year went on. Sickly grass under it, raspberry canes settled against the loosely joined wooden steps Nickel had built, one surviving straggle of morning glories curtaining the bathroom window, high weeds clinging to her legs if she ventured off the path that led from the door. In the heat, everything seemed hostile. Too green, too blue, too yellow, buzzing, stinking. Food spoiled, the sweat that stained her clothes smelled rancid. It was very difficult to keep Stevie clean. Sometimes she left the trailer in the middle of wiping and dressing him and ripped up handfuls of grass or prickly plants, wrenching and tearing, hoping to take out her cruelty on the weeds instead of him. There was something rote in the way she did this, as if she was performing a scene of a woman at the end of her tether, but that was part of what steadied her.

"You won't dump me, Lady?" he asked once, when she came back inside.

"Dump you?"

"Dump me somewhere."

"Why would I?"

He smiled at her too-forceful tone, as if he could see through her. She was irritated. She wanted him to know she was honourable. She wanted to know it herself.

"But you could, Lady."

"But I won't. I'm not like him."

She'd regretted saying that when he looked away, not smiling. Nickel had told her that she didn't know when to shut up, but he'd laughed, admiring, like it was special or sexy, brave.

Stevie looked back at her, reluctantly forgiving. "Thanks."

"No worries." She punched him on the arm, which he couldn't feel.

—

"Lady" was what he'd called her when he first met her. "A lady is coming to see you," Nickel told him. "A nice lady. She's my new friend." *Hi lady*, Stevie said when she came in the door, holding a book about owls and a toy car behind her back. Nickel was disapproving later: you can't buy a child's love, he said, as though she thought you could. She'd painstakingly earned Stevie's love. "Lady" became her name.

—

They lived on a flat stretch up a slope from the road. The car was parked at the end of the driveway (Nickel had taken his motorbike). She couldn't see the car from the bedroom window and imagined someone stealing it, waking in the morning to find herself marooned. Her nearest neighbours were the Michaels family, foul-mouthed, noisy, nosy, friendly. They frightened her. On the other side, an immaculate old couple in a bungalow. She and Stevie probably frightened them. Neither house could be seen from her front door.

Behind the trailer, the woods were dense and silent, the ground covered with pine needles and spindly bushes that caught at her clothes. There was one path, overhung with hemlock. The path twisted suddenly, branching off a few feet into the trees. In summer, buttercups grew wild right up into the shadows. In winter, the snow bent the branches lower, so it looked like a doorway, the wolf's mouth of a folk tale. She didn't go in there now, she didn't really go anywhere except to get groceries or to bank Stevie's disability cheque and her welfare payment. She imagined Stevie with no one to call for help, shouting himself hoarse.

When she first moved in, Stevie had been little, but old enough that the trailer had felt very small, his child's mind watchfully alive to adult currents. She and Nickel would go into the woods at night, just where the path curved out of sight, near enough that if Stevie woke and yelled, they would hear him. They could still see the light on in the kitchen, through the gaps in the branches, but they themselves had vanished from the world, the trees swallowing them up.

Farther down the path was the Memorial Tree. When Nickel told her he was taking her to see it, she'd assumed a tree he had planted, perhaps with a plaque underneath like the ones in parks, and wondered at the privacy, the discretion, that had made him choose such a secret place. But the tree was a massive pine, easily among the tallest, and there was no discretion to it. It was a work of living art, Nickel told her, and she agreed. The trunk was carved with designs. Faces, letters and numbers, Celtic knots. He'd stripped the lower branches, driven nails into the bark. Framed photographs and objects hung from hooks. Each photograph was of a person he had known who had died, some close to him, some only intermittently thought of, and the objects were things that had belonged to them, or that he felt they would have loved. Pens and clocks and cooking pots, jewellery, toys faded by the rain and snow and air. A small drum. A car key. One earring. A wind-up plastic bird, orange bleaching into dirty white.

Nickel had lost a lot of people. Both parents and one brother, as well as a number of hard-living friends. He'd lived on a commune up to age six, watched over by an old man whose death had left his parents so orphaned and aimless they'd carted him and his three brothers around the continent, always looking for a place like the one they'd lost but never staying anywhere long enough to find one. There was always something wrong with where they'd landed, and they kept moving. No wonder he was so good at leaving.

Low down the trunk, almost at the roots, she found a photograph of a young woman in a plaid shirt and jeans, squinting against the sun, maroon hair growing out and showing brown streaks, one hand to her cheek, plump fingers stiffened with silver rings.

"But she isn't dead."

"What?"

"His mother isn't dead, she's gone."

Nickel shrugged.

Now she thought sometimes about adding to the shrine. A memorial for Nickel himself. Photograph, some intimate object. Old toothbrush? Stained T-shirt? A nest of hair from his comb?

She also wondered now if others represented on the tree were really dead, or only gone. Living elsewhere, unaware of their symbolic passing.

Either way, she had not gone back.

—

She wrote:

I have been pondering the meaning of prayer.

It was morning. Coffee on one side, crumbling toast on the other, smears of butter along the keys, Stevie still asleep. He slept more than she would have thought possible, worn out by boredom and by the shock of his new, unaccustomed existence. He was crossing into another way of living, and it made him very tired. She could not sleep.

Outside, birds fought and squirrels warned each other in the trees. Every thing, every living thing, fights for territory.

She wrote:

As a child, I held a literal faith. I was raised in a Catholic household and sent to Catholic school. I believed as a child believes. Prayer for me was a reward system, as though God was another teacher. If I prayed hard enough, if my soul was pure enough, God would

answer my prayer. When my dog ran away, I prayed that he would come back. When he did, I thought it was because I had prayed good prayers and was being rewarded for my goodness.

When I was nine, my mother was diagnosed with breast cancer. When she started chemo, I prayed. When she had to stay in the hospital, I prayed. When my father, unable to handle the crisis, left our family, my brother and I prayed together, every night in the backyard. When my mother died, I thought it was because I did not pray hard enough, or well enough, and God was punishing me for praying badly. It took me years to see how egotistical this was, as though my mother's life and death depended on whether or not God thought I prayed good prayers!

It took me a long time to understand that prayer is not a protection against suffering. We do not pray to be spared, we pray for the strength to bear whatever it is we suffer. However, it took my brother's accident for this to be true for me. I now understand prayer in a new way. This trial has brought me closer to God, and closer to the fact of Christ. I am thankful.

Her mother was not dead, she was in BC, and her bout of cancer had cost her only a few incisions. Her father had not left, unless you counted his habit of silent staring, as if he'd successfully found a sanctuary inside himself in the middle of everything: her mother's verbal floodgates, her admonishments and postures, the chattering world.

She didn't believe in God. She wished she did. People who did fascinated her. Nickel did, in a way: some version of God had been part of his childhood, far more than hers. Even if it came to nothing, he'd had belief. She wanted belief. It would have been helpful to have someone to speak to, other than Stevie, to whom she could be hurtful or petty or inadequate. God could bear that weight. Stevie was not a person who could bear any kind of weight anymore.

In the third week, some people began to post comments. She'd set up a comments section almost as a dare when she started her blog after weeks of reading Catholic websites late into the night. She wanted to be offered a pure sympathy. Sympathy was comforting and potentially useful. There was no one currently in her life from whom she could ask for such sympathy. She'd moved here to be with Nickel, and Nickel had moved here to get away from people and left to get away from Stevie. When she decided to stay with Nickel, she'd thought she wanted to get away from people too. Now she wanted people, but no one she actually knew, because they knew her as herself—shy, not always truthful, envious of whatever she was not, stupid about men. She wanted to be Sister Bernadette. She wanted witnesses to her transformation into this uncontaminated and noble suffering being.

And then, like magic, the witnesses arrived, posting comments. Guileless, faceless, mysteriously full of love.

Hi sister I just want to say I feel what you feel my son is in a wheelchair for 3 years and I don't know what to do sometimes but with GODS LOVE I am strong thanks for sharing.

I was really interested to read what you wrote about your mom its what happened to me too. I'm not really catholic but it really meant a lot to me to read what you wrote.

I am sending you all of the LOVE and BLESSING of CHRIST. "I am the way, the truth and the life, no-one may come unto the FATHER, but by me."

Emoticons. Pictures of sunsets. Kitschy crosses on top of a green hill. Christ's wounds. People emerging from the dark swirl of nothing into which she was sending words.

She tried to feel guilt, then told herself that these people, whoever they were, took heart from Sister Bernadette. Sister Bernadette, who struggled but did not doubt, who might feel rebellion but did not blindly fear the dark, the futuristic green glow of the digital clock reading 4 a.m., and outside, the wind bending the indifferent trees.

Hi Sister Bernadette,

I've been reading your blog for a while and I wanted to tell you I really admire it. I am especially moved by your comparison of your own path to your wish to walk the Camino. I myself have walked the Camino twice, once as a young man and again two years ago (just after I retired).

I'm curious. Would you consider posting a photograph of yourself? It would give your readers someone to picture behind the words.

Best,

Leonard

—

She didn't write anything for three days. She turned off the computer. It sat in the corner, the dead black of the blank screen reflecting her as she moved around it, tidying, making their cursory meals. She tried not to think of Sister Bernadette as she struggled to position Stevie so he could shit, or wiped the smell from under his arms, or tried to find a DVD he wouldn't refuse from the pile in the broken laundry basket by the TV that she'd moved to the end of his bed, or sprayed lilac air freshener in a cloud over his head, Stevie assuming his tolerant, absent smile. But on the fourth day she sat down abruptly, pressed the power button.

Hi Sister Bernadette,
I hope I didn't offend you. I would just like to see what you look like. I only meant that it would help your readers to get a sense of the person behind these posts.
   Again, I hope I haven't offended you.

Dear Leonard,
Of course not, but my brother has been even more unwell these last few days, and I haven't found the time to write. I often feel selfish, nattering away on my blog when he might need something! But now I am back.
   Best,
   Sister Bernadette

Dear Sister,
I am glad. So, what about a photograph?

—

She spent an hour looking at stock photographs of nuns. Old women, smiling with their lips shut, younger women looking straight at the camera with calm eyes. Evil nuns from old films, leering at novices or with stiff vengeful jaws. Nothing seemed to fit, and the risk was too great. She'd have to take a different risk. It needed to be a photograph of herself.

She drove to Walmart and bought needles, thread, black and white cloth. She bought nothing else, nothing for Stevie, no food, she didn't invent an excuse for the time, the gas. She paid cash and threw the receipt in the garbage, so she couldn't change her mind and return everything. It was too late for that.

As a child, a teacher read her classroom "The Wild Swans." She loved the story—the lost girl who can't speak, the nettle shirts that sting her hands to pieces, the enchanted brothers turned to swans, the prince who loves her beauty and her sorrow, her holy silence, the last-minute reprieve when the wood that will burn her bursts into red roses. She wanted to be filled with secret virtue, condemned and then saved. Her goodness revealed, a goodness that would confound the world and shame anyone who had doubted her. She remembered the story as she sewed herself a scant habit, just enough cloth to cover her head and over her shoulders—the photograph would show only her face. She pricked her finger on purpose.

She pinned it in the back, and pulled out the full-length mirror from behind the couch. She used to keep it on the door, to check herself before she went to work (tending bar in town, quit now for Stevie), but Nickel took it down.

"What the hell?"

"It bugged me."

"It's mine."

"You don't need it."

"I do need it. I need to know I look okay before I go to work."

"Use the bathroom one."

"That one's no good."

"You look beautiful. You're beautiful. You shouldn't worry so much."

"I'm not *worrying*—"

"It creeps me out, I keep seeing myself when I'm trying to paint." He kissed her. "Just stand in front of me, where I can see you."

She hung it back on the nail, wondering why she hadn't before, and faced herself in the mirror.

She looked preposterous. It was too large and billowy around her face, too tight across the forehead, someone dressed up as a nun for Halloween. But she adjusted, she pulled and tucked, and looked at herself for a long time and was happy. Her sliver of a face, pale now from being mostly indoors, the dark spatters of her freckles, her long narrow nose, seemed to her graceful and refined, with the corkscrews of her hair hidden. If she smiled with her lips closed, like the older nuns in the pictures, it hid the tobacco stains on her front teeth. She smiled at the face she wanted.

Behind her, the reflected room. Brown couch with seams of white where the fabric had worn, like a stuffed toy with an eye missing. Curling posters. For a painter, even a bad one, Nickel's taste had been strangely bland—Van Gogh's sunflowers, Monet's water lilies, gold explosions of Klimt. Unless he'd just hoped to make the room pretty. Grey linoleum with pink swirls like dirty ice cream, a sheet over the window, two hard chairs and the coffee table, laminate mahogany pressboard peeling at the corners, so marked with overlapping rings from hot or wet cups that it looked like an intentional pattern. There were some marker scribbles and pictures low down on the wall, sharp squiggles of blue and black made idly by a maybe six-year-old Stevie, streaks of yellow and red made in deliberate provocation age eight, and some kind of landscape, made in an effort of improvement at age eleven. There was a river with a boat full of people, some disproportionate swans, a pale-green island crowded with carefully drawn trees. She'd always planned to repaint the wall. Now she was glad the drawings were there.

—

She stood on the front steps in the full sun and took a stream of pictures, positioning herself so the door filled the background, neutral, not obviously a trailer. She wanted her readers to imagine a bungalow with a wild garden or, even better, a lopsided log cabin, smelling like baking bread, woodsmoke. What she herself, while still in Nanaimo, had imagined a life on a sideroad near a small Ontario town to be like. More like a story of a life.

—

She wished she could show the pictures to Stevie. They were so good. She hesitated between three. In one, she was almost frowning, thinking deeply, looking to one side. In the second, she smiled very slightly, her eyes steady on the viewer, and in the third, her smile was broader, almost jolly. In the end, she chose the second one—it balanced lightness of spirit with gravity, as Sister Bernadette did.

Today I posted a photograph of myself, as requested. It took me a long time to pick one—it looks like I am not as free from vanity as I would like!

I have had a difficult time in the last two weeks. I miss my life in the Order, I miss the presence of my sisters, the feeling of common life and common purpose. The routine, too. Burdens are easier shared. My brother has been very unwell, and I am his only support and only caregiver. Money is a constant worry. Rent, food, heat for the winter. Even living simply, as we do, we are always close to real want. Another spiritual test for me, I know, but sometimes it feels like the opposite. These worries and fears draw me away from Christ. I just have to keep believing that God provides, and that when we are lowest, we are closest to Christ. But I am selfish and afraid, and sometimes near despair over how my brother and I will continue.

I've been thinking about the scallop shells that pilgrims on the Camino road used to wear on their cloaks. Now I'm told they sew them on their jackets, or wear them around their necks on strings, or just keep them in backpacks, out of sight. There are legends surrounding why the scallop shell is important in walking the road to St. James, but whatever else it is, it is a metaphor for pilgrimage. The ridges of the scallop shell are all the places from which the different pilgrims come, the journeys they must make to get on that road, but all the roads lead to the same destination, like the way the ridges meet at the base of the shell. I think this meeting isn't only the meeting of pilgrims at the end of the road, but the meeting at the end of life, the great meeting we prepare for.

—

Stevie had a bad night, waking her again and again to complain that he hurt in places where he couldn't hurt. She knew about phantom limb pain, but couldn't believe it happened when the limbs were still there. Like her, he'd grown sallow. She couldn't carry him out into the yard, though she would open the window in the afternoon so he could feel some of that yellow warmth, watch the sun travel across his body. She'd briefly arranged for a nurse to help (she could get one visit a week for free), but Stevie hated the woman so much that she'd asked her to stop coming, and the region was too thinly populated to find another nurse quickly. They were on a waiting list. Their lives were waiting lists. He stayed in bed.

Stevie was handsome in a slight, slippery way. When a child, he rarely wanted to be held or kissed, which suited her fine. Now she knew his body almost better than she'd known Nickel's. She'd cared for it, worried over bedsores, turned him this way, that way. Cleaned his teeth, his ass. Yet even with that, he was still politely unreadable, waiting until she left him alone.

"We can't stay here, Lady."

She was feeding him a bowl of soup, more as a way for both of them to pass time than because he was hungry. It was the middle of the night. She'd taken the clock away at his request. He said he stared at it too much when he woke up, brooding over the slowness of the minutes.

"Where would we go?" She lit a cigarette. "Want one?"

"After you."

She ground hers out on the windowsill. Lit a new one, and held it to his lips.

"Smoke it yourself."

"I can smoke after."

He sighed. "Lady. I love you."

"I love you too."

"But I am not your fucking charity case."

"Go fuck yourself."

"Can't reach my dick."

After a pause, she spluttered laughter and he did too and they both laughed longer than they needed to.

She smoked the cigarette.

"What if we got an apartment in town? Like a ground-floor one? Or somewhere else? You could get a job again, maybe, we could have some more money, get different home care, not that fucking Nurse Ratched, a breath-operated wheelchair—"

"There's no money to move with. This is it."

"Can we sell the land?"

"I don't even know where the deed is. He probably took it. And it's all in his name, everything, everything here is his. He would have given it to you or me when he left if he wanted us to have it."

"Then we have to get some money, Lady."

"There's no money," she repeated. "There's nothing."

They stopped talking. She finished her cigarette.

"You still want one?"

"Sure. But give it to me, and then light it. I don't want your spit on it."

She put it between his lips, lit it. He pulled deeply and exhaled out the side of his mouth.

When the ash got too long, she took it and knocked it on the windowsill. He spoke to her back.

"Lady."

"What?"

"I'm gonna die here."

—

He finally slept. She lay down beside him on the bed, watching his face, smelling his sour night breath. Thought about what would happen to him if she disappeared. Thought about the expression "gone to ground," meaning hiding. Hiding in the landscape. Hiding and never coming back. Gone to ground. Gone to earth.

—

I don't know where you get OFF but this whole thing is such a fucking scam who are you morons reading this pity party and crappy hallmark pseudo catholic MUSINGS you are obviously some kind of bullshit con artist people like you are disgusting playing on religious fantasies well RELIGION IS THE OPIATE OF THE MASSES SO WAKE UP

She'd expected this, but it still shook her. To have so much indiscriminate hate directed at her, from someone who went looking for an object of scorn, and yet she knew it was true, and, being true, almost fair.

—

She started to wear the habit when she sat down at the keyboard. When the light came in from the right angle, at a certain hour in the afternoon, the screen reflected her face as she wrote, and the cloth hung low enough that she couldn't see her T-shirt, her jeans and bare feet. Sister Bernadette furrowed her brow, concentrating, writing, reading, responding. A person of faith. Her mother used to say that, "a person of faith," as though there was nothing else to be said, that such a person could fearlessly be trusted, or loved.

———

Dear Sister Bernadette,

What a splendid photograph. You are younger than I expected.

I just wanted to say "Keep your chin up," about some misguided people posting unkind comments. You know this, probably better than I do (I have a short fuse!), but it's better to forgive and not dwell on those kinds of things. People like that (and you know who you are!) just go through life looking for an excuse to mistrust.

As I said before, it's good to be able to picture your face. I really do take great comfort from reading your blog. My wife sleeps in Christ and our two children live very far away (Tokyo and Dubai, believe it or not!), so I sometimes get grumpy, from being alone so much. Reading your blog makes me feel less alone.

Best,

Leonard

Before, his profile had been a picture of a handsome older man, grey-haired, slightly prim around the mouth, with red traces in his small, tidily cultivated beard. A fussy, intelligent man, she imagined, who took walks, read, tried unsuccessfully to talk to strangers. Now the picture beside his note was of a scallop shell.

—

Dear Leonard,

I agree! Though I would add that, in Christ, we are never alone. But it's hard to remember, at times (without struggle we wouldn't be human, I guess).

Thanks for the scallop.

Dear Sister Bernadette,

Of course (but as you say, hard to remember). I'm glad you liked the scallop.

I think I've been struggling because teaching (my former profession) is so social. You are always "on," and there is always something to do, someone who needs you. (I taught at quite a rough school outside Kingston, rural poverty is really astonishing.) Even after three years, it's hard to adjust.

Thanks for helping.

Best,

Leonard

Hi Leonard,

I know exactly what you mean. For most of my adult life I've lived communally, working together in a common purpose. I'm needed now, very much, but it's hard to remember that this new life is also full of purpose. That what I do is still seen by God.

Maybe that's why I dream so much of the Camino de Santiago—that sense of a clear purpose, and a common goal. I pray about this, daily—that I will be able to find purpose and continue strong in my faith, no matter what my situation is, and that material want and a life of service is what I chose willingly, only in a different form.

May I say, with gratitude, that I pray for you?

Best,

Sister Bernadette

—

Without his picture (he kept the scallop shell), she imagined him more, adding detail that the tiny square would not convey. Height (tall, a little stooped, as Nickel had been), heavier than he'd been when young, with a light, almost fey voice, precise pronunciations. Carefully kept hands (her own hands were roughening, stung with small cuts, and her nails chewed down), wearing round gold-framed glasses when he read. He'd subscribe to things, send his children slightly querulous emails about news stories and opinion pieces. Have strong feelings about books, but still spend a lot of time at a screen, chasing online theories down that amorphous expanding trail. He'd chop his own wood for his fireplace, but know that those days were numbered. He'd be sensible about things like that, his good judgment another form of masculine bluster. A woman would come and clean his house every two weeks. He would stay out of her way, make admiring comments as she left. He would send Christmas cards with genuinely funny things written inside.

—

Outside Kingston was not far from her. Had he mentioned it half on purpose, some kind of unconscious overture? And if so, to what?

Unless, like Sister Bernadette, he did not exist.

—

Dear Sister Bernadette,
Would it be possible to ask you to send me an email? I have
something I must ask you. Please believe me in advance that I
have thought this through carefully.

    Best,
    Leonard

He'd put his email address below. Her address was her name
(her real name). She made a new one as Sister Bernadette and
sent it to him. The password was his name. She waited.

—

Dear Sister Bernadette,
I really appreciate the trust this shows in me. I will get right to
the point.

    I would like to pay to send you on the pilgrimage.

    You would have no obligation to me in this.

    I respect your privacy. We would not even need to meet.

    I have done some research. Your airfare, equipment (you need
walking gear!), food, the cost of a good professional caregiver for
your brother while you're gone, plus food etc. for him. $20,000
would be ample. I am in a position to offer this.

    Would you do me a favour and consider it?

    Best,

    Leonard

—

She sat on the front steps. They were more wobbly than usual; she realized she was shaking. She did calculations in her head. First and last on a decent apartment in town, someone (not a professional someone, a strong teenager would do, she could pay one of his old friends, even) to look after Stevie when she was at work, how many months' rent it would cover while she saved money, money accumulating for the first time, maybe an evening off now and then, she would go for a walk, she would take herself out to dinner, she would drive herself to a movie, and they'd still have his disability payments, and she could find a social worker to help her with the tax credits and subsidies she didn't understand. Maybe they could move farther. To another town where no one knew them, where no one would find them.

The trailer would stay, surrounded by the wicked squabbling of forest creatures, raccoons would invade, she'd leave the door unlocked, she would leave everything to ruin. If Nickel came back, they'd be gone. He would stand in the open doorway, the door off its broken hinges. Unable to believe she'd done something without him.

—

Dear Leonard,
I am overwhelmed by this offer. I can't accept it. I'm sorry that I must have given such an impression of desperation. I thank you, from the bottom of my heart, but I can't even consider it.

You are a good man. Thank you.

Dear Sister Bernadette,

Let me say a few things.

I have never, for a second, thought you were asking for money. Your story moves me, and gives me strength. That, in itself, is a gift. This is in thanks for the gift. I know it seems like too much, but it isn't. Practically speaking, I have substantial savings, a good pension, a house with no mortgage, and my independence, God willing, for some years still. My children both have very good jobs and make no demands on me. This is something I can afford to do. This is something I want to do. Let me do it.

Best,

Leonard

—

She went into Stevie's room.

"Are you awake?"

"Yeah, now."

"I think I found some money."

"Online gambling?"

"I'm serious."

He opened his eyes. "Where?"

"Don't worry about it."

His cheeks were pink.

"Want to move?"

He turned his head to the window. He didn't want to show his longing.

The sun was rising.

She could see him deciding not to ask.

Maybe he would never ask.

This is what it feels like to save someone's life, she thought. I never knew.

—

Dear Leonard,

I have struggled with this over the last few days. I could not decide whether it was pure selfishness in me to want to accept your offer. But, after much thought, I believe that your goodness in making this offer will balance out my selfishness in accepting it.

Yes.

I don't know what else to say.

Yes.

Thank you.

Dear, dear Sister Bernadette,

I am so pleased.

If you send me your address, I will send a cheque.

She hadn't considered this. Her name. Her place. He would have to trust her, and believe her, even more than he already did. She didn't know if he loved Sister Bernadette enough for that.

Sometimes, when she woke up in the night, she suspected she'd been dreaming about the road, the real road, she'd feel the heat and the packed earth trodden by thousands of feet, as though the Camino wasn't something she'd found mentioned online as a Catholic pilgrimage site around which she could make a story. As though she, or Sister Bernadette, were really going. As though that was what she really wanted.

—

Dear Leonard,
Here is my address, and the name for the cheque. I use my old
(former) name at the bank in town—I grew up here, and this is
the name the old manager still knows me by. I feel very strange
about this name. It's not mine anymore. I am not that woman
any longer. But here it is.
   Bless you.

She could be found now, if he wanted to find her. The same
means that had allowed him, in the largeness of his free time,
to find the writings of Sister Bernadette would probably locate
pictures of her real face, her real house, in seconds. He would
have to love Sister Bernadette very much not to wonder and
search and begin to suspect. He might even find the local story
about Stevie's accident, with her name in it. No mention of nuns.

   Of course, he could easily not be who he said he was, either.
Lying awake, she imagined a man coming up the path, sweep-
ing a flashlight before him, stumbling to her door in the dark,
knocking, then breaking glass. Malignant, searching, nothing
that she thought.

—

Or a call from the police. A mortified old man, his capable and
vindictive children, a minor news story, shame.

—

Or silence. Just silence. Days, then weeks, then months. She
would, she knew, take a long time to give up. On the money

and their escape, but also on his goodness, his belief, which allowed her to feel that Sister Bernadette really existed. Not a hoax, but a source of light.

She would pray in her despair, even if it was the crass and desperate prayer to be spared pain, not the reasoned prayer that asks only to bear with dignity. Dignity was for people like Sister Bernadette, or like Leonard himself. She would pray at night, prostrate, waking Stevie. She would tell him everything. He would curse her. He would be right.

—

Shame. No matter what happened, shame.

—

The cheque came in a card with white roses on the front. Thick, off-white paper, scalloped edges, the envelope lined with silver. Perhaps an old card he'd found in his desk, maybe something that his wife had bought once, pretty, blankly feminine. Had he hesitated, embarrassed, wondering if this was the right gesture?

There was nothing written inside. Not even "best wishes," something frustratingly generic. She couldn't believe he would send no message. She looked in the envelope again, hoping for something she'd missed. Wondering what he believed, what he'd guessed.

His writing on the cheque itself was the scrawl of an impatient man, his signature illegible. A blue ballpoint, the ink patchy. And the cheque so slight, see-through in the sunlight. Nearly nothing. She smelled it, along with the card. No particular scent. No trace at all, of anyone.

—

She wrote: *Thank you.* Sat and tried to think of something else to add, but there was nothing. He didn't answer, and she didn't write again.

—

She took the cheque to the bank. The money appeared. She would make plans as fast as she could. She looked at pictures of apartments in larger towns, where it would be easier to find Stevie what he needed, to find herself a job she wanted. She sat at the edge of Stevie's bed and they looked at the pictures on her phone, giddy with their future. When he fell asleep, she'd check her bank balance, amazed that the money was still there.

—

A different town. She would be a different woman. They would be, as much as they could be, saved.

—

Sometimes, very late at night, she would sign out of her bank account and light a cigarette and feel such loss, such sorrow. Not guilt, sorrow. For Sister Bernadette. She put her hand over her mouth, bereft.

—

She would hang the habit from the Memorial Tree.

—

He would come to find her. She was sure. In a few months, in a year. It would be too much for him. There would have been no more messages from her, no fake photographs of Sister Bernadette in airports or walking down the pilgrimage route. She would not be guilty of that. It would be more honourable to simply disappear. He would have confided in no one, least of all his children or the police. Who wants to look like a fool?

—

He would park in the empty driveway. He would avoid the empty trailer, the cold ooze of it, smashed windows, open door, trash and hated furniture, the pile of Nickel's paintings, piles of tin cans, Stevie's mural bubbling and streaked from driving rains. It would be a sunny day, afternoon. Solemn, golden. He would walk down the path, ducking under the boughs. He would find the Memorial Tree and sit under it for a long time, looking up at the only thing left of her, limp on the branch, protected from the wind.

Piss and Straw

NAOMI COULD NOT BE MADE TO MOVE FAST, SHUFFLING in her slippers by the reception desk, under the eyes of the staff. Trout allowed herself to see covert approval in the faces of some of the nurses and PSWs, as if they believed that what she was doing was, according to how her mother had lived and how she would wish to die, right. It was wishful thinking; they didn't know what Trout intended. They didn't know much about her mother's life one way or another. They didn't have time to ask, and if they had, Naomi didn't know, anymore, how or what to tell. Trout didn't know much about their lives either. She tried not to imagine their lives too much. Imagining what is not freely told had come to seem to her like a form of intrusion.

The border would be closed to non-citizens in twenty-four hours. The highway was nearly empty, the border guard strangely unconcerned, waving them through after only a few questions. Trout took this as a sign that her course was blessed, while knowing it was due more to injustice and luck: a middle-aged white woman, judiciously dressed in a rental car, a sleeping ancient beside her, colliding at just the right moment with the guard's indifference or distraction.

But they were through.

Trout kept driving, letting herself breathe more deeply. Naomi remained asleep.

Trout hadn't told anyone she was coming. She wasn't even sure how she would, whether they had a phone by now, where she would find a phone number. She could have written a letter, but there was no time for that. And she didn't want to risk a likely refusal. Or worse: finding there was no one there at all. She'd convinced herself that someone was still there. She wondered if she was insane, or just hopeful.

She aimed for the town nearest the farmhouse, trusting that memory would take her the rest of the way. She'd known every road and path once. She'd known nothing else.

When she was a child, crossing into Canada with her mother, they'd stopped at a motel restaurant, the first time she'd been in a restaurant of any kind, and ordered eggs. Naomi kept up a nervous patter so Trout wouldn't ask questions, but Trout didn't want to ask questions. She'd been too entranced by the pallor of the yolks, shivering and then breaking under her fork. The eggs she'd collected with Strawberry in the henhouse had deep-golden yolks, almost orange. She'd never seen industrial eggs. There were so many firsts still to come, but she hadn't known that yet. First high-rise, first escalator, first subway car, first time she saw the hook of water that came when you pressed the button on a drinking fountain. She poked at the eggs and they shone, reflecting the lamp above the diner booth. Naomi smiled at her. She had not told her daughter where they were going, or that they would never go back.

Well, not never, Trout thought, wondering if there was any way to find the diner, if there was any chance the diner was still there.

To the staff, she'd only said her mother was *going home*. It wasn't a lie. She'd often felt that the aridness of her mother's life after leaving the commune had to do with her mother's decision to abandon the leaking farmhouse in the woods, her home as very few modern people, Trout believed, had homes. In her more resentful moments, she believed her mother had taken away her own capacity for being at home, even though she knew it was childish to be a woman in her forties who still blamed her mother for her own skittishness. That part of aging terrified her: the possibility that, rather than attaining wisdom and detachment, she would find herself more and more obsessed with a past she could not alter, railing at her mother in her mind the way a small child kicks the legs of the parent, demanding and demanding and never satisfied.

This idea of taking her mother back had come to her before the lockdown or the notice about the border's impending closure, but it was the extremity of those things that made her act. Everything Trout thought of as normal had been suspended, including the things she had regarded as fundamental decencies. Why shouldn't she also do something dramatic and unimaginable, like take her mother back to the place she'd been most herself and leave her there?

Naomi had spoken very little for five years, but in the last few months she'd said, when she saw Trout arriving, *go home*. Pointing at the door.

"What?"

"Go home."

"Go home?"

"Go home. Go *home*."

Her bottom lip out-thrust, finger quivering, her other hand pulling the sheet to her chin as if she was naked under it.

"What do you mean?"

"Go home."

Trout had first taken this as *go away, I don't want to see you*. She'd stayed, though she joked with friends and with her ex-husband that it would have been a relief to take her mother at her word. But she didn't. Of course she didn't. She sat and held her mother's hand. She tried to follow the thoughts she believed her mother had, charting the spasms of her face.

Over time, she changed her mind and took it as an entreaty, an impossible wish. It made sense for Trout to try to give her mother what she wanted: she'd been perversely dutiful all her life. Her mother, when she got an idea into her head, could not be persuaded otherwise. And, Trout thought, this was a way of having her cake and eating it too, carrying out her mother's last request and being free of her at the same time.

She had told very few people about her plan. Her half-brother had argued and then given in, sighing into the phone in a way that made Trout angry, as if she was behaving like their mother. She was, but not in an identical way; she suspected her brother liked to classify things in order to digest them, that she and her mother might fall, in his mind, into a category of *women*, though she couldn't blame him much, neither of them had been easy. But she guessed her brother might be relieved, her proposal absolving him of a responsibility he didn't want and could barely afford. The care home was expensive, and Trout, who barely managed her small apartment, was not in a position to help with the fees, on the understanding that she helped with everything else. Afterwards, he could always say he'd misunderstood. Maybe it was true.

She did not tell her ex-husband. He would have tried to talk her out of it. He'd been amused by Naomi before her dementia had set in, was secure enough in himself to be amused by how narrow she found him. He was very difficult to provoke, though Naomi tried. He'd even loved her. But that was over now, that was what divorce meant. You no longer owed each other explanations. He was not the person she owed an account of herself to. She didn't have such a person.

She could have told Strawberry. She'd even composed an email.

I am taking my mother to your mother.

Then she erased it.

I am going to see your mother. Do you have anything you want me to say to her?

She erased it.

I am giving my mother to your mother.

She erased it.

The Maine roads were almost empty. She supposed everyone was sheltering in place. The rest stop she'd pulled into was closed.

She had to take her mother into a field, persuade her to squat beside a fence post. The cows on the other side ignored them. Naomi refused to get up again, sat back into the beaten-down and now wet grass. Trout kicked at the earth, half dragged Naomi back into the car, strapped her in. Slammed the door, thought bitterly that it was obviously for the best that she had never had a child. Naomi glared at the cows as they drove away. Trout glared at the road. Both of them smelling of piss and straw.

Pissing in a field was one of the few memories Naomi had relayed about Trout's father. They'd driven back to Toronto, to steal some things Naomi wanted from Naomi's parents' house. They waited across the street until her parents left, found the key under the mat, and took jewellery, the money that was kept in the broken teapot above the sink. Trout's father, Mattie, was amazed by the house, the slovenly capaciousness of it. He watched as she rifled through drawers, left what she didn't want on the floor. Watched as she considered whether or not to leave a note. And then she didn't. She let her parents think they'd been robbed.

Driving back into Maine, they'd stopped for her to squat in a field and she'd wet her long skirt. She'd danced, swinging the skirt, and she'd felt Trout kick inside her, the skirt arcing out as she spun, the world spinning, the baby kicking, all that cosmic certainty, the rightness of her life.

Trout had no memory of her father, who'd left in the night only a year later. Younger, she'd imagined him dead, that that was why he had never tried to see her. *Full fathom five thy father lies/Of his bones are coral made.* As if he was floating in the depths below her, just outside where her mind could reach.

Her mother, like her father, had left the commune in the night, though Naomi had taken Trout with her. Returned to Toronto, accepted money from her parents, made herself a life. Trout had made herself a life too, an orderly one, domestic, modest, though apparently a life that could be kicked over at a stroke as she became a woman who, in the middle of a pandemic, strapped her afflicted mother into a car and took her back to the woods.

> *The awful daring of a moment's surrender*
> *Which an age of prudence can never retract*
> *By this, and this only, we have existed*
> *Which is not to be found in our obituaries*

Her mother liked to quote that at Trout, long ago. It was one of the things John used to say to them, standing on the stump in the field from which he preached. Trout was due, she thought, for her own moment of awful daring.

Go home. Go home.

Naomi slept again, the houses dwindled, and the roads were familiar and strange at the same time. Trout thought about her awful daring, and the houses and whoever was in the houses, and the question of how to die. When her mother had been diagnosed, when she and her brother had decided she must be put into care, when she had more or less given up speaking, Trout had worried over this question, but the way she might worry over a small argument with her husband or a lost object, missed but not essential. Now she didn't have a husband and the doors of care homes would be locked and the borders closed and the question of how to die had exploded in her hands, or in her mother's papery blue-veined hands (how had her hands aged like that? when?). Not as an abstraction, but the particular question of how this person Naomi was meant to die, and where, and what Trout owed her. The consensus, both of the government and of the general population, seemed to be that Naomi was owed a stringent and antiseptic safety, without touch, without sunlight or company or anything Naomi herself would recognize as a life. She was owed the kindliness of no visitors and enhanced cleaning measures, which, Trout suspected, was also a mirage. The reality would be desertion, the old dying alone in untended corridors. But even if Naomi could have been isolated in perfect comfort with every need of her diminished body immediately met, that was not how her mother had wanted to live, or intended to die, insofar as she was capable of intending anything.

Go home.

The farmhouse was inhabited, as far as she knew, only by Strawberry's parents, Sarah and Charlie, and a man called Saul, who made clay bells they sold in local gift shops. The last time Strawberry had checked, that was who remained. Later, Strawberry, under the influence of a slightly disreputable therapist, cut off all contact with her parents for good. That was years ago. It was possible that Trout would find the house deserted, shutters and doors banging in the wind.

When Trout was a child, she'd helped Saul knead the clay he dug out of the riverbed, watching his face to see if she did right. His face was scarred, his hair tied back with blue string.

He'd told her stories: of his Mexican mother and his white father, who lived with his family in another city. He visited, told Saul he loved him. When he turned eighteen, Saul went to his father's house. His father said he didn't know him, and did not interfere when his wife called the police as Saul stood disbelieving in the yard. Then the war. Then back to America, his face scarred. John had found him sleeping in a parking lot. John had promised him a new heaven and a new earth. John had renamed him Saul. His mother had named him Paul, after his father. John told him it was not his name. He was Saul, always on the road to Damascus.

Trout could not imagine Saul old.

She imagined the farmhouse more or less unchanged, though falling in on itself, and the faithful trio, each winter biting more cruelly into their bones. They too were presumably mulling over the question of how to die. Of what a good death was, which led from the question of what a good life was. Trout muttered to herself, steering carefully in the dusk, *global health crisis*, *global emergency*, *global pandemic*, and these phrases, the way they were employed, seemed to show a willingness to adhere to mere life, to bare life, stripped of any meaning beyond biological continuance.

It was nearly dark. But she found the way just as she'd hoped, brought the car to a halt in the driveway. She left the headlamps on, hoping someone would see them and come out. She thought of herself sitting at the farmhouse table, the table crowded, bodies pressed together for warmth. That alien child, who'd remade herself so completely that the person she was until age ten had vanished from the world. The child who swam during thunderstorms, whose body itched with small cuts, who climbed so high the branches bent under her, who knew how to build and tend a fire, what plants could be eaten or put on a bruise. Trout wasn't sure she missed that child. She was used to being embarrassed by her, in the sense of something extra, something useless, that she carried around because she'd found no place to set her down.

A door opened and a figure lumbered into the headlights. She carried a stick. Trout couldn't tell if this was for defence or support. She was stout, a man's brown coat falling open, a scarf wound around her sparse hair.

I am taking my mother to your mother.

"Yes?"

She sounded wary, though not afraid.

I am giving my mother to your mother.

Trout opened the door.

"Who are you?"

She got out. "Hello, Sarah."

The woman drew back. "Who are you?"

Trout went to the passenger side, got Naomi out of her seat. Presented her. She fought the urge to smooth her mother's hair, untwist her skirt. Instead, she went back to the car and turned off the headlights. Sarah came towards them in the dark.

"Oh, sweet merciful Christ," Sarah breathed. She put her hand to the side of Naomi's head.

"She doesn't talk anymore," Trout said, "she won't recognize you."

"Oh, she knows me. She'd know *me* anywhere," Sarah said, and Trout resisted telling her this was not true.

As Naomi and Sarah looked at each other, Trout wasn't sure what was or wasn't true. Maybe Naomi did know this woman, this place, and Trout pictured leaping into the car, driving away. She could. She could go to a motel, sleep, drive back across the border in the morning, a citizen returning.

"Come on, then, come, come inside," Sarah said, and Trout took Naomi's hand and they followed Sarah up the path, walking carefully over the uneven earth.

When Trout was a child the house had been overfull, shouts on the stairs, a chaos of coats and boots in the closet by the door. The house, a red wood rectangle of the nineteenth century, looked like a ship foundering, the spatters of light in the kitchen window making the rest of the house ungainly, as if it was sinking crookedly into the earth. The smell of the kitchen: ferment of old food, sweat, dirty dishes, hemlock and pine needles tracked in, swept out again, tracked back. The cellar, jars of preserves in rows, halved fruit and chopped vegetables under the sweep of the flashlight. Trout and Strawberry played a game of walking across the cellar floor in darkness, feeling along the swollen walls. Their hands floured with earth from the places where the masonry gave way. Cobwebs and snarls of dust in their hair. Feral, cocksure in their kingdom.

This nearly dark house.

Her mother did not stumble on the path.

Before she opened the door, Sarah turned, bending to Trout, fingering her lapel. Trout could smell her breath: untended teeth, herbs. Sarah had always chewed herbs for toothache.

The smell was stronger than she remembered, a body edging cumbersomely towards death. A big woman in a purple dress, leaning on her walking stick. Her face cracked like dry clay.

"I like your coat, honey," she said.

There was no light in the hall, just the flicker from the open door to what they'd called the Commons, the big room with the stove around which, in the depths of winter, everyone slept, laid together for warmth, their breath hanging in the air. Naomi, recalling that time to Trout once they were in Toronto, described herself as desperate. Her back pressed against another knobby, half-starved back, Trout against her front. Feeling Trout's cold fingers, the reddened tip of her nose. Staring out at the precepts stencilled on the walls (*philosophers have hitherto interpreted the world; the point is to change it*) and the Doc Sinclair lyrics (one of the few people whose songs they were arbitrarily permitted to sing) and thinking she could not stay here, that her child was so thin she could feel the skin contracting between her ribs. But Trout remembered her own body infused with the warmth of others, protected from the cold outside, the long stakes of ice hanging from the eaves glinting in the moon, and then deep sleep. Sometimes Strawberry beside her, whispering, and the smell of wool and dirty cloth and the banked fire. The wood stove smoked, a thin blue haze seeping from the chinks in the stovepipe.

The room was larger than she remembered, perhaps because it was so bare. There had been books, though only books of which John approved (he'd enjoyed burning books he thought were harmful, and Trout had helped him do it, reverently placing them in his hands and so into the stove, where they'd smouldered, the cloth-bound covers refusing to catch). Now the shelves were almost empty, and a bare bulb glowed feebly overhead, not the candles she remembered. She felt cheated by the big room. It was her right of adulthood to find it shrunken, scaled to a manageable size. She shivered, even with the heat coming off the stove.

"Look what the cat dragged in," Sarah called, standing back with a flourish of her hands to show Trout and Naomi.

The two old men sitting in wooden chairs on either side of the stove turned. Charlie, his strong body lumpen, a visible tremor in his hands, one eye milky. Saul, grey-haired, still using that ratty blue string, scrawny except for his belly. The piece of wood and the knife he was holding clattered to the floor, a second too late for her to believe it spontaneous. He stood, steadying himself on the back of the chair, and that too seemed calculated, though not to any purpose Trout could guess, unless it was to buy time to absorb what he saw. She'd once asked him if he was her father, and been disappointed when he'd laughed, though gently, because he was always gentle with her. He would let her pound the clay but not touch the glaze, sitting in metal bowls on the long work table under the trees, a blue tarp slung above for when it rained. Poisons stained his hands. Pearly white, gradations of blue, yellow, red like thinned blood or the sap of an unknown tree, and, used sparingly because it was so expensive, gold. When it was her turn to go barter for groceries in the nearby town (whoever went usually took a kid, the grocer couldn't bear the sight of their thin arms, it was easier to talk him into taking a load of firewood instead of the money he was owed), she'd catch sight of the bells sitting in a squat row in the window of the gift shop. It hurt her heart to see them looking so dull and ordinary when Saul was so beautiful, a giant who could throw her up over his head so her hands touched the leaves on the trees. It was Strawberry who'd grown up to be a painter, and Trout envied her paintings, which hinted at the beauty of those glazes, shining in the sun.

Saul came and kissed her cheek, and she breathed chemicals and cannabis and sweat. He went to Naomi, who shrank back against the door, her mouth pursed, her hands up to defend herself.

"She doesn't recognize people, Saul," Sarah said authoritatively, "she's not well."

"Would she recognize us anyway?" Charlie asked, not moving from his chair. "She's been gone for forty years."

"Thirty-five," Trout said.

Charlie grinned unpleasantly. He would not forgive Naomi, Trout thought. He would not forgive anything. His life had been too hard.

They sat on the big couch, which had been covered and recovered so many times it was a patchwork of blue, grey, brown fabric scraps. It sagged under them. Trout and Naomi in the dipping middle, Trout self-conscious, hating the way she was dressed, the neat jacket, the zippered boots. Sarah and Saul on either side, Sarah's thigh jostling Trout, Sarah's face impossible to read. Charlie stooped and picked up the whittling knife and the stick from the floor, offered them to Saul, who shook his head, and then began hacking at the stick himself, long shavings falling around his feet.

"What are you doing here?" he asked. The knife slipped.

Naomi sat up. "Go home," she said.

Sarah leaned across Trout's lap and took Naomi's hand.

Trout could not tell, and so didn't want to ask, how much they knew about the outside, which in her time had been carefully rationed. With John long dead and only these three, maybe that wasn't true anymore, with the world so freely available, streaming relentlessly through the air, renewed every second. She wasn't brave enough to take out her phone and see if she had a signal.

"Can we stay?" she asked. She hadn't meant to ask. She'd meant to proclaim her plans with such force that no one would contradict her.

Sarah kissed her, missing her cheek and hitting her ear. "Never thought I'd see either of you again," Sarah said, and that seemed to be an answer.

She slept on a mattress on the floor beside her mother's bed, in what had been the room they'd once shared. Trout listened to her mother snore and watched the moon through the branches and tossed and turned, worrying about bedbugs, worrying that it was her own body, and not the house, that was diminished.

She got up early, not sure how much she'd slept. Naomi could sleep till noon. Trout eased herself off the mattress, her knees drawn up to her chin on the hard ridges of the braided rag rug. Again thought of how easy it would be to slip away. Outside, there was only a light scrim of snow. The roads would be clear.

In the kitchen, she found Saul getting breakfast. He moved ponderously, eyeing the jar of granola before lifting it from the shelf, measuring the milk into a cup before pouring it into the bowl. Saving his strength, saving the food.

"Old age isn't for sissies, Trout," he said, as if this had never been said before.

She put the jar back on the shelf. "Is it okay that we came?"

He looked at his hands. She'd forgotten that no one was allowed to answer a question quickly, to indulge in reflexive politeness, and wished she hadn't spoken.

"With me. It's okay with me."

He chewed slowly, making each scrap last, licked the bowl while she wondered if she could tell him she loved him, whether that would comfort what must be an intolerable isolation or whether he would know it wasn't true, couldn't be true, that she felt love looking at him because it was more companionable than fear, considering her own folly, thinking she would find a place for her mother in this house. Someone had painted a dark red eye over the door that led upstairs, which she'd missed last night in the dark, whispering her mother along the hall, feeling the places where the wallpaper had loosened, bubbling with damp.

He set the bowl down. "He knew, he was right," he said.

She didn't know what he meant.

"He prophesied all of this," and he nodded with immense satisfaction, "he knew we would bust ourselves up, we would just fall apart. He always knew. And now it's happening."

It must be nice to be proved right, Trout thought, as he washed his bowl out at the sink. She wasn't sure what she knew, or whether the pandemic and what would result from it was as final as he claimed. It could be. Or it could be another disoriented step, faltering but not disastrous, not in the sense Saul and everyone she'd grown up with had meant and even wanted. Signs appearing in the sky, sure as a star in Bethlehem. Something that would turn the course of the world.

Outside, away from their rarefied stale air, she'd come to feel that history was not so decisive. That everything that pulled one way also pulled in the other. She looked at Saul's stooped back. Joke would be on her if he was right, if this was the blow from which no one recovered, the chaos that would swallow them. Perhaps he'd feel vindicated.

Sarah and Charlie came in, measured out their portions, ate. Neither seemed inclined to speak, though Sarah, getting up to go to her loom, touched Trout's hair the way she used to when Trout ran past her towards the door.

They did not offer her food.

"I have to run an errand," she said to Sarah. "Can you keep an eye on Naomi while I'm gone?"

It was peculiar to drive into town instead of walking along the shoulder, hauling an old wagon. It was like watching a sped-up film. She passed the place where Sarah and Naomi had sold Saul's clay bells at a folding table by the road for the few tourists who drove by and stopped. They would elaborately braid their hair, put on long bright dresses kept clean for the purpose, benign feminine hippies smiling, radiant and vague. *Better dress up for middle America, kid,* Sarah would say, whickering like a groom over Naomi's braid, both of them gloating afterwards, cash gripped in Sarah's hands, how they'd flirted with the men without insulting the women, throwing a brief shine over them, but not too much, just enough for an interlude. *The double act,* Sarah said, counting. Trout and Strawberry watched their mothers, proud.

Trout remembered the co-op in town as a somewhat dismal outfit, occupying the ground floor of the town's only office building, a plate-glassed fifties low-rise, the modernist structure promising a future that never arrived. Now the entire building was co-op, gleaming in the sunlight. Squares had been taped on the pavement for where to stand and wait to be let in. A young woman in a mask stood at the door, clicking off entrants on a counter, her eyes anxiously bored over the white mask. Trout found her square, stood with her hands balled in her pockets, shivering. Other than the lineup for food, the town was apparently empty, and Trout could study how it, like the co-op, was changed, without anyone thinking she was staring at them. Yoga studio cheek by jowl with hunting and fishing supplies, the café advertising organic coffee, the dour, darkened pawnshop. The evangelical church she'd remembered appeared to be gone now, and she felt a sadness, remembering it was one of the places she'd been most curious about, considering whether the people handing out pamphlets about damnation had anything in common with her own sense of separateness. Wrought iron lampposts stood in the corners of the square. The metal curlicues evoked the nineteenth century, but the lampposts hadn't been there when Trout was a child. She wondered about the one hotel, once the summer home of a lumber magnate, and built according to his haphazard impression of an Italian villa, with slabs of oak as stand-ins for stone, slightly buckled, white paint fading grey, repainted every few years. A rich man's wish for a more splendid place, betraying a fretful hunch that this place was not real.

The town was real. But it was hard to feel it was when it was so empty, more like something dreamt, a dream that held herself as a child, walking with her head down, fearful of the imaginary malice of strangers (they were not allowed to talk to strangers), not as she was now, an unobjectionable woman feeling for her keys in her pocket, waiting to buy food at the beginning of the end of the world.

The co-op, when she was allowed inside, was silent, the people seeming to avoid eye contact, not sure how they were supposed to behave. A few old men and women greeted each other loudly, hugged. Trout waited till the aisles were empty, not from fear but from a wish to avoid offending. She looked at the racks of bread and buns, tables of every kind of fruit, rows of preserves and honey on the shelves. It was ludicrous that this could exist, with the treed hills rising behind (the whole back wall was glass). Even if the entire edifice crashed down, the improbable part was that it was there at all, this profligate American abundance. Thinking of Saul measuring out his milk, it seemed impossible that this place existed. She could stretch out her hand and grasp any kind of food she fancied, load a cart. Astonishing, absurd.

Sarah must come here; Trout could see a row of bells beside one of the checkout counters. Thinking of Sarah standing in this opulence, bartering with the staff, Trout was reminded of Strawberry's stories about East Berliners after the fall of the Wall, wandering the aisles of newly revealed grocery stores with empty shopping carts, unable to afford more than one chocolate bar or a few apples.

Trout had rehearsed what she would say if Sarah asked about Strawberry. Yes, she's okay, yes, she has a life she wants. Ways Trout could be kind or reassuring, eliding the obvious: your daughter will not come back. She does not want to see you. She does not want to speak to you. She has decided this. You will never be in her presence again.

She loaded the cart furiously, grabbing things from the shelves. Sacks of rice and flour, sugar, dates, honey, packages of nuts. Unable to stop, she added things she was sure they didn't even eat. Cheese, canned beef stew, twenty packages of pasta, three bags of hot cross buns. She took out her credit card before she could change her mind, trying to ignore the total. She didn't care, she knew it was grandiose and condescending and trying to absolve herself of something she couldn't define and she still didn't care.

She loaded the car and realized she was very hungry and needed coffee. There used to be a bakery across the square, and there still was, and it appeared to be open, a man leaning on the counter, no one inside.

The bakery, like the town, was changed. White laminate and fluorescent strips replaced by Edison bulbs and uneven slabs of dark wood. The pastries were expensive lumps, glowing through the window, the breads irregular shapes with rough crusts, the cakes pale cylinders on circles of silver cardboard. The scene wavered. The window glass was rippled. In her memory, the glass was smooth, the fluffy white bread in rows; she'd turned to look at the bread, wondering what it tasted like, Naomi pulling her hand. She recognized the man behind the counter, she thought, though he'd have been a teenager then, probably the son of the owner. He smiled at her politely as she approached, not sure of the protocol, sure he didn't recognize her, and pointed at a croissant and asked for coffee.

He'd seemed much older than her, but he wasn't anymore, not really. He was greyed and fleshed out. Not fat but florid, with a bright-eyed attentiveness. There was a photo on the wall behind him, showing him with his arms around a boy and a girl. He'd never left. Or he could have come back here to live only recently, after years away, moving his resentful urban family to this town, his parents failing. The prospect of a new chance, a new life that no one in his family had planned, though he was the only one who wanted a new life. She could see the wedding ring, tight on his slightly swelled finger. The renovation would have been his idea. Going upscale for the tourists, for the times, the pressboard and harsh lights outmoded. He would lose his business, without tourists. She wanted him to remember her.

"Do you need anything else, ma'am?"

"No, thank you."

"Take care now. Take good care."

"You too."

"Holy shit, kid, we'll never eat all that!"

"Try."

Trout and Sarah stood in the storeroom, looked around at the boxes and bags. Sarah took out a package of crackers, ripped off the cellophane with her teeth. Then she sat down hard on a three-legged stool in a corner and ate the entire package, staring at Trout as a squirrel with a nut stares. She crumpled the rest of the packaging in her hands.

"I forgot how plastic catches the light." She held it up.

Trout expected a lecture now: warming oceans, the Pacific garbage patch, the horror of what was to come, maybe the same apocalyptic complacency as Saul, with his fixed stare that Trout remembered and later recognized in photographs of veterans, their eyes vacant as marbles. But Sarah wondered at the package like a child with a soap bubble. She put it in her pocket. Got up and handed Trout empty jars, dragged out bins from under the long counters.

"Okay, let's get busy or the mice will be in everything." She opened pickles, ate one meditatively. "I make my own, you know."

"I'm sorry, I didn't mean—"

"Mine are better."

Trout nodded, struggling with the thread that sealed a brown paper sack of flour.

Sarah handed her a pair of scissors. "I sat with her all night, when she was in labour with you, kid," Sarah said, and Trout looked down, daunted by how she spoke, expecting something in return. "Rubbed her back and then we walked up and down up and down up and down with Mattie on her other side. You sure took your time. We prayed and we sang."

Some of the flour had spilled over the lip of the jar.

"Did she say why she left?"

Trout shook her head, then knew that was the wrong thing. "She said she was wasting her life," Trout said.

Sarah tucked her chin to her chest, considering. "She wasn't patient, was she? And I love her. I love her as much as I ever loved anyone. I lost a baby after Strawberry. She's buried out back, you remember. And it was your mother who got me through that year. Charlie wasn't up to much. But I don't think there are any wasted lives. I've lived a faithful life, here. Maybe it didn't work out how I hoped, but I was faithful. Followed my prophet into the woods, tried to get myself right. Stayed when you folks took off, stayed when John passed on, and then when everyone left and it was just the three of us, stayed with Charlie even though he's a mean fuck. So it didn't work out like I thought it would, so that's not my business. The point is to be faithful. You think the people who listened to the Sermon on the Mount weren't idiots, kid? Just wasting their lives? I will be buried out back and whoever is here can nail a cross over me and that will be the end and I will have been faithful. Naomi wasn't faithful. If she was she'd have stayed and now I'd walk this ground with her and I'd sit with her till she died and I'd wash her body and bury her out back where I'll be buried too and that seems like a pretty good way to go. What else does she want?"

Sarah had heard John, her prophet, preaching in a park in Pittsburgh, where her father was a steelworker. She'd worn, she said, a pink dress. Plump, acned cheeks, stopping to listen, transfixed.

"Can I leave her here?"

Sarah stopped, sat back on the stool. "Dumping your garbage, yeah?"

"Can I?"

A silence.

"That's a big deal, kid, what you're asking. She's not a cat."

"I know that."

"I'm thinking on it."

Trout put the food away as best she could. Sarah thought aggressively, hunched, her chin in her hands.

That night, they ate pasta that Trout boiled and then she went and sat in the snow and watched Saul making bells under the tarp, his hands slick and grey with slip-clay. Saul, in his over-large duct-taped coat, could have been thirty years younger. Agile, hostile, loving her. She sat on an upturned crate, the snow melting when the flakes touched her bare hands.

She could see Naomi and Sarah, sitting together at the table in the kitchen, Sarah talking, Naomi touching her own face with one hand experimentally, as though her hand might find there was nothing there.

In the morning, Trout took Naomi walking. She wanted to get out of the house and let them talk without her. She didn't know what Sarah had told them, or if Sarah could just decide, the way Trout had decided to return, or Naomi had decided to leave. How had the habit of decision taken root after John died, after so many years of never having to make any decisions? Trout kept her mother close as they walked slowly through the frozen ruts of mud into the thicker trees. She imagined Naomi abruptly collapsing, falling into the mucky leaves and patches of snow. Sarah could help her to bury her. She would not have left her mother, her mother would have left. It would be a good death. Or an ending.

She didn't know what would make a good death, only what would not. There was that obituary phrase, *in accordance with her wishes,* and she looked sidelong at her mother, who was muttering, her free hand clutched to her chest, and Trout thought of a woman she'd stood beside in an elevator, a bald patch worn into her grey hair, her hands working together, saying over and over *your iniquity your iniquity your iniquity your iniquity,* how the woman seemed to be trapped within those words, like a mouse fallen into an empty oil drum. She didn't know what her mother's wishes were, she could only guess.

They came to what Trout thought of as their destination, where an old hunting lodge had once stood. One room with a cot in the corner, the sheets falling apart when touched, moths rising from the pillow. One of Strawberry's paintings showed two girls crouching on the floor. Trout disliked the painting, though she did remember hiding there with Strawberry when they were children, she wasn't sure why.

The lodge was gone. The boards must have been taken away over time, maybe used by Saul for firing the kiln. There was a square marked by four big stones that had secured the frame, and some bits of wood from old window sashes, spangles of glass here and there in the moss. Nothing else. Trout found herself more troubled than the loss deserved. As if she had thought her past was waiting for her, intact. She didn't believe in resolution, though she must have, in some way, or she wouldn't be standing staring at the four stones, trying not to panic.

Naomi's expression changed. She's wet herself, Trout knew from experience. Trout wished there was someone to tell this to, who would find it funny: the lodge, the memory, her mother's wet skirt, the other memory, Naomi dancing in the field, with the cows and the stars and Mattie, who hadn't known how soon he would go.

Trout coaxed her back along the path, Naomi's hands folded over the wet stain. She found Sarah hacking at her garden beds, clearing away the shining brown rot of the winter.

"Oh, honey," she said, leaning on the shovel, "come inside and I'll get you fixed up."

They took her into the Commons, led her to the couch.

"You sit tight," Sarah said.

"Do you have something I can put down under her?"

"Don't be squeamish, kid. It's just clean piss."

Naomi leaned her head back on the couch. Trout sat beside her as Sarah bustled out, shouting into the yard.

Saul and Charlie came in with an old tin bath, painted red with a white stripe, dented and rust spotted, followed by Sarah, holding metal jugs.

"Are you serious? She'll freeze," Trout said, as Sarah ran the water.

"Oh, no, she'll be fine. We got a tank put in a few years back. It's hot already, feel. She'll like it. She needs a wash, not a wipe down. If it was summer we could take her down to the river. She used to jump in the river as soon as the snow was gone, right around this time."

Trout was distracted by Naomi wriggling away from her and onto her feet. She looked down at herself: green cardigan and grey dress, the darker wet spot at her thighs like a map. The only sound was the slosh of water as they poured jug after jug into the bath, steam rising.

She slowly unwound herself from her cardigan, dropping it on the floor, and before Trout could get up, she'd lifted her dress over her head, rolled down her underwear and kicked them backwards. Saul hooted and Sarah slapped her thigh.

"That's it, kid," she said.

Naomi raised her arms, reaching for something over her head. Crinkled armpit hair, the rolls of her belly lifting, a collage of contrasting textures, wrinkled and smooth, soft and rough, reddened around her neck and hands, silvery along her torso. She stepped jauntily into the bath and sat down.

Sarah poured the first jug of water over her, holding it high above Naomi's head. She spluttered, slapping her palms on the skin of the water, only a few inches deep. Saul, Charlie, and Sarah took turns, handing off the two jugs in a line. Naomi shut her eyes against the flow that streamed over her hair, along the shrunken stretch between her breasts. They poured water over her until the room was full of steam and the bath overspilled, puddling on the floor.

Sarah went to the cupboard and pulled out a faded egg-white towel, handed it to Trout. "That's your mother," Sarah said, as if Trout was in danger of missing something, this room her last chance.

Trout lifted Naomi under the armpits, moving timidly, afraid of hurting her, made more nervous by her audience.

Naomi struggled under the towel, knocked back into her own childhood, unless she had become Trout and Trout Naomi, drying her daughter's hair with mildewed towels in their basement apartment in Toronto, both of them wondering what would happen next.

Trout looked up at Sarah, who nodded.

"Yes?" Trout asked.

"That's your mother," Sarah said again.

Trout left the next day, before she or anyone else could change their mind. Naomi stood beside Sarah on the front steps of the house, Charlie and Saul on the porch above them. Four old people and an old house, dead vines suckered to the windows, some of the broken panes patched with cardboard, the door open but nothing visible inside because of the slope of the porch roof, the unlit hall.

Four people.

Then three.

Then two.

Then one.

Then just the house. It would stand. It takes a long time for a house to fall in.

Trout looked back at the end of the driveway before she turned onto the dirt road that would lead to the paved side road and the highway. She waved.

Naomi raised her hand. Not waving. More like a signal, her fingers held open to show Trout her hand was empty or to show her she understood or thought she understood. What could Naomi understand? That Trout loved her? That Trout would not come back?

When Trout was out of sight of the house, she stopped the car and got out. The sky was grey. She hoped it wouldn't snow. She wanted to look for the gap in the trees, off the main path, down which Naomi had carried her, half-asleep, to where she'd hidden the car on the night they left. She couldn't find it. It must be completely grown over now. Of course it was. Trout stood, listening to the cold silence all around her. The empty trees, the empty road, the sky. Then she got back into the car and headed home.

Acknowledgements

Some of these stories appeared, sometimes under different titles, in *Joyland*, *The Malahat Review*, *The New Quarterly*, and PRISM *international*. Thanks to the editors. "The Crooked Man" also appeared (as "The Bride and the Street Party") in *The O. Henry Prize Stories 2017*, edited by Laura Furman.

Work on *Householders* was supported at various points by the Canada Council for the Arts, the Ontario Arts Council, and the Toronto Arts Council. I am very grateful.

Quotations in the text are from The Incredible String Band, William Blake, T. S. Eliot, Shakespeare, and the Port Huron Statement.

Just as I was editing this collection, March 2020 happened. I was partly supported that spring and summer by the Canadian Writers' Emergency Relief Fund and the Woodcock Fund. The money meant I was less anxious as I moved commas around.

Thanks to everyone who administers the fund, and everyone who donated to it. I was a better writer, spouse, and parent.

Thank you to my agent, Barbara Berson, who works tirelessly, offers excellent suggestions, listens patiently, and talks me down from ledges.

Thank you Dan Wells, for being my ideal editor.

Thank you to everyone at Biblioasis for all your work, particularly Vanessa Stauffer for answering my questions, even silly ones.

Thanks to my parents, Jutta Mason and David Cayley, my mother-in-law, Veronika Ambros, and my sister-in-law Ruth Ambros.

For friendship and ongoing conversation, thank you Anna Bekerman, Adrienne Connelly, Jenny Cook, Kate Kaul, Jessica Moore, Alayna Munce, Julie Petruzzellis, Simone Rosenberg, Mayssan Shuja-Uddin, Kilby Smith-McGregor, Souvankham Thammavongsa, Jane Wells and Amy Withers.

Thank you to McMaster University and the Hamilton Public Library, where I wrote early drafts of many of these stories.

Thank you to everyone at Artscape Gibraltar Point, where I finished them.

Thank you to my neighbours, Jesson Moen and Denise Santillan, and their son Oscar, for their friendship with our family, which helped us through the roughest patches of 2020.

Thank you to my wife Lea Ambros, and our children, Livia, Tom, and Danny, for all of it.